PAPERCUTZ SLICES

THE HUNGER PAINS

PAPERCUTZ SLICES

Graphic Novels Available from PAPERCUTZ (Who else..?!)

Graphic Novel #1
"Harry Potty and the Deathly Boring"

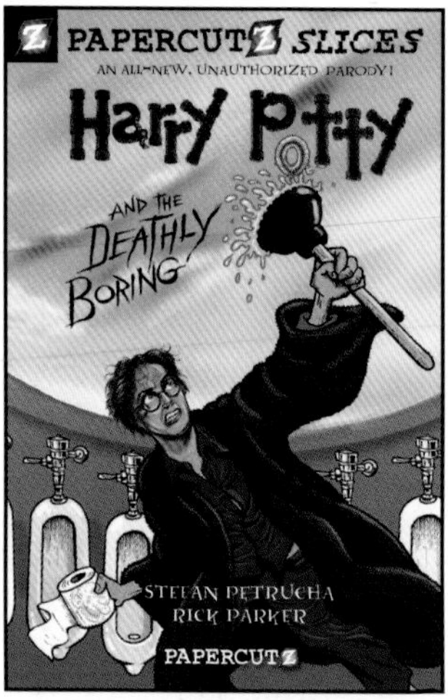
PAPERCUTZ SLICES
AN ALL-NEW, UNAUTHORIZED PARODY!
Harry Potty
AND THE DEATHLY BORING
STEFAN PETRUCHA
RICK PARKER
PAPERCUTZ

Graphic Novel #2
"breaking down"

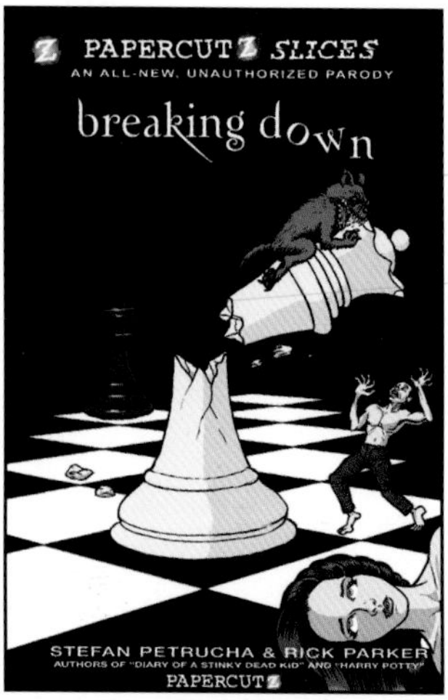
PAPERCUTZ SLICES
AN ALL-NEW, UNAUTHORIZED PARODY
breaking down
STEFAN PETRUCHA & RICK PARKER
AUTHORS OF "DIARY OF A STINKY DEAD KID" AND "HARRY POTTY"
PAPERCUTZ

Graphic Novel #3
"Percy Jerkson & The Ovolactovegetarians"

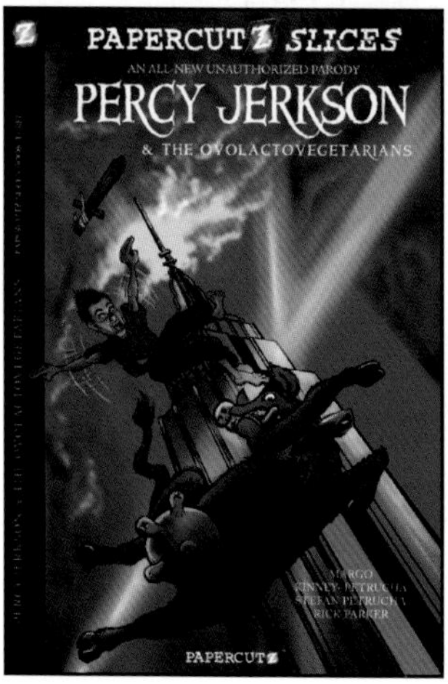
PAPERCUTZ SLICES
AN ALL-NEW UNAUTHORIZED PARODY
PERCY JERKSON
& THE OVOLACTOVEGETARIANS
PAPERCUTZ

Graphic Novel #4
"The Hunger Pains"

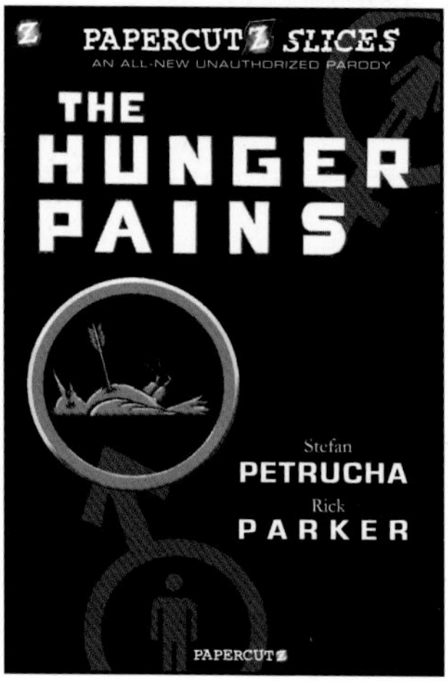
PAPERCUTZ SLICES
AN ALL-NEW UNAUTHORIZED PARODY
THE HUNGER PAINS
Stefan
PETRUCHA
Rick
PARKER
PAPERCUTZ

NEW! PAPERCUTZ SLICES is now available from COMIXOLOGY

Now you can read PAPERCUTZ SLICES and look like you're conducting serious business!

PAPERCUTZ SLICES graphic novels are available at booksellers everywhere. At bookstores, comicbook stores, online, out of the trunk in the back of Rick Parker's car, and who knows where else? If you still are unable to find PAPERCUTZ SLICES (probably because it sold out) you can always order directly from Papercutz—but it'll cost you! PAPERCUTZ SLICES is available in paperback for $6.99 each; in hardcover for $10.99 each. But that's not the worst part-- please add $4.00 for postage and handling for the first book, and add $1.00 for each additional book. Going to your favorite bookseller, buying online, or even getting a copy from your local library doesn't seem so bad now, does it? But if you still insist on ordering from Papercutz, and just to make everything just a little bit more complicated, please make your check payable to NBM Publishing. Don't ask why—it's just how it works. Send to: Papercutz, 40 Exchange Place, Ste. 1308, New York, NY 10005 Or call 800 886 1223 (9-6 EST M-F) MC-Visa-Amex accepted

www.papercutz.com

PAPERCUTZ SLICES

#4 THE HUNGER PAINS

Stefan
PETRUCHA
Writer

Rick
PARKER
Artist

New York

"THE HUNGER PAINS"

STEFAN PETRUCHA – Writer
RICK PARKER – Artist, Colorist, Letterer

NELSON DESIGN GROUP, LLC
Production

MICHAEL PETRANEK
Associate Editor

JIM SALICRUP
Editor-in-Chief

ISBN: 978-1-59707-312-7 paperback edition
ISBN: 978-1-59707-313-4 hardcover edition

Printed in China
February 2012 by New Era Printing, LTD
Trend Centre, 29-31 Cheung Lee St.
Chaiwan, Hong Kong

Distributed by Macmillan
First Printing

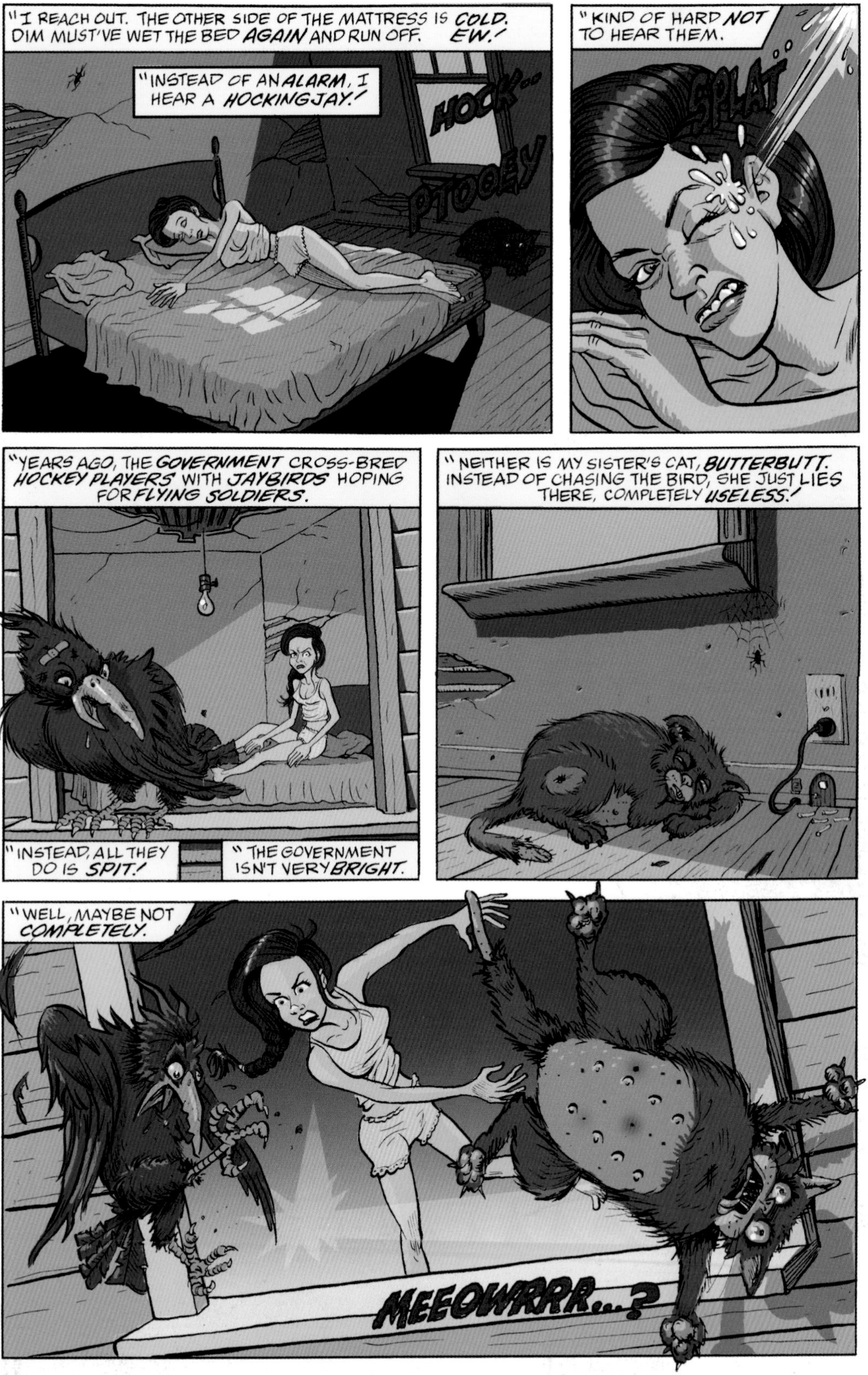
"I REACH OUT. THE OTHER SIDE OF THE MATTRESS IS COLD. DIM MUST'VE WET THE BED AGAIN AND RUN OFF. EW.!
"INSTEAD OF AN ALARM, I HEAR A HOCKINGJAY!
HOCK...
PTOOEY
"KIND OF HARD NOT TO HEAR THEM.
SPLAT
"YEARS AGO, THE GOVERNMENT CROSS-BRED HOCKEY PLAYERS WITH JAYBIRDS HOPING FOR FLYING SOLDIERS.
"INSTEAD, ALL THEY DO IS SPIT!
"THE GOVERNMENT ISN'T VERY BRIGHT.
"NEITHER IS MY SISTER'S CAT, BUTTERBUTT. INSTEAD OF CHASING THE BIRD, SHE JUST LIES THERE, COMPLETELY USELESS!
"WELL, MAYBE NOT COMPLETELY.
MEEOWRRR...?

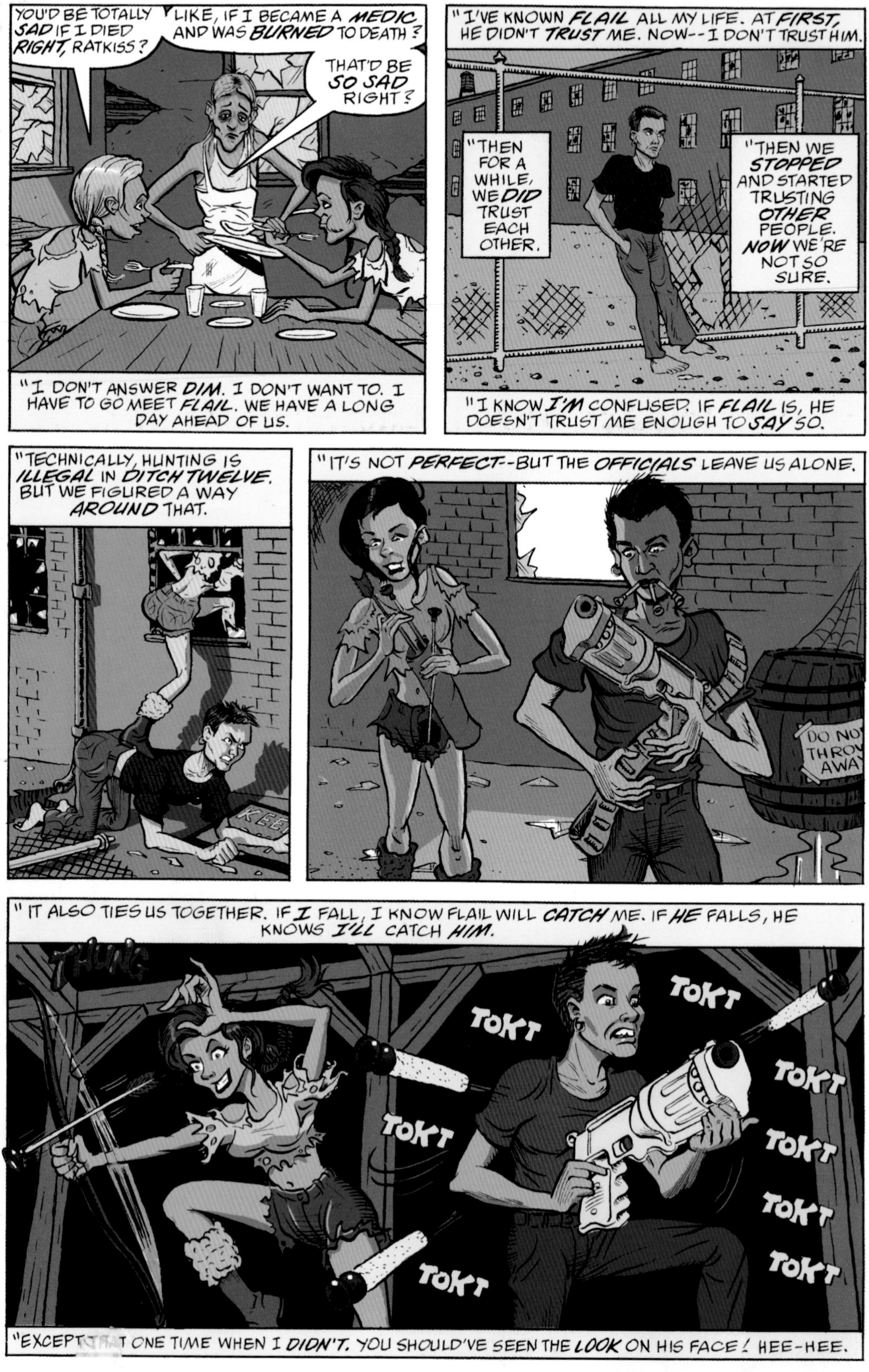

YOU'D BE TOTALLY SAD IF I DIED RIGHT, RATKISS?
LIKE, IF I BECAME A MEDIC AND WAS BURNED TO DEATH?
THAT'D BE SO SAD RIGHT?
"I DON'T ANSWER DIM. I DON'T WANT TO. I HAVE TO GO MEET FLAIL. WE HAVE A LONG DAY AHEAD OF US.
"I'VE KNOWN FLAIL ALL MY LIFE. AT FIRST, HE DIDN'T TRUST ME. NOW-- I DON'T TRUST HIM.
"THEN FOR A WHILE, WE DID TRUST EACH OTHER.
"THEN WE STOPPED AND STARTED TRUSTING OTHER PEOPLE. NOW WE'RE NOT SO SURE.
"I KNOW I'M CONFUSED. IF FLAIL IS, HE DOESN'T TRUST ME ENOUGH TO SAY SO.
"TECHNICALLY, HUNTING IS ILLEGAL IN DITCH TWELVE. BUT WE FIGURED A WAY AROUND THAT.
"IT'S NOT PERFECT--BUT THE OFFICIALS LEAVE US ALONE.
DO NOT THROW AWAY
"IT ALSO TIES US TOGETHER. IF I FALL, I KNOW FLAIL WILL CATCH ME. IF HE FALLS, HE KNOWS I'LL CATCH HIM.
THUNG
TOKT
TOKT
TOKT
TOKT
TOKT
TOKT
TOKT
TOKT
"EXCEPT THAT ONE TIME WHEN I DIDN'T. YOU SHOULD'VE SEEN THE LOOK ON HIS FACE! HEE-HEE.

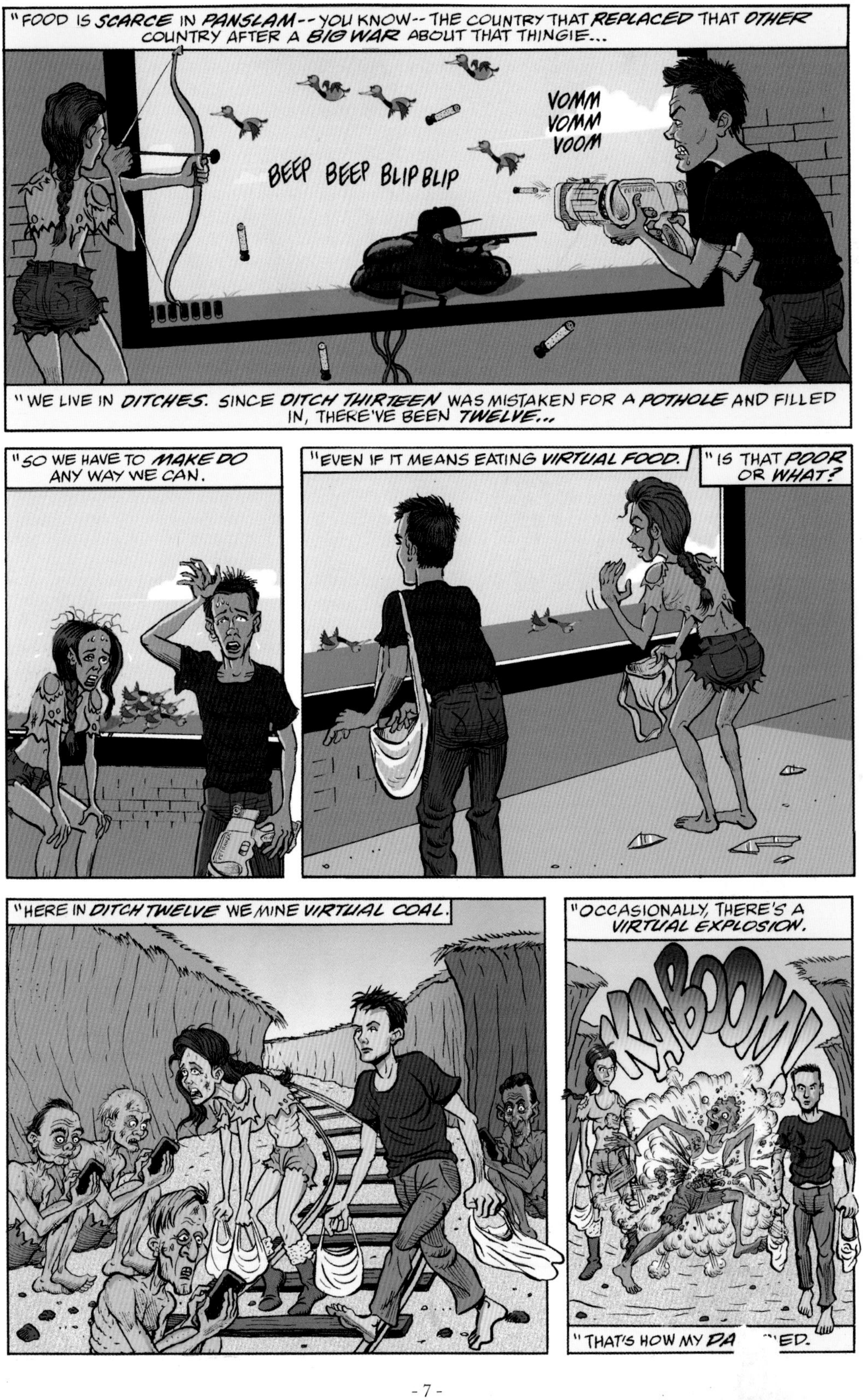
"FOOD IS SCARCE IN PANSLAM -- YOU KNOW -- THE COUNTRY THAT REPLACED THAT OTHER COUNTRY AFTER A BIG WAR ABOUT THAT THINGIE...
VOMM VOMM VOOM
BEEP BEEP BLIP BLIP
"WE LIVE IN DITCHES. SINCE DITCH THIRTEEN WAS MISTAKEN FOR A POTHOLE AND FILLED IN, THERE'VE BEEN TWELVE...
"SO WE HAVE TO MAKE DO ANY WAY WE CAN.
"EVEN IF IT MEANS EATING VIRTUAL FOOD.
"IS THAT POOR OR WHAT?
"HERE IN DITCH TWELVE WE MINE VIRTUAL COAL.
"OCCASIONALLY, THERE'S A VIRTUAL EXPLOSION.
KABOOM!
"THAT'S HOW MY DA ED.

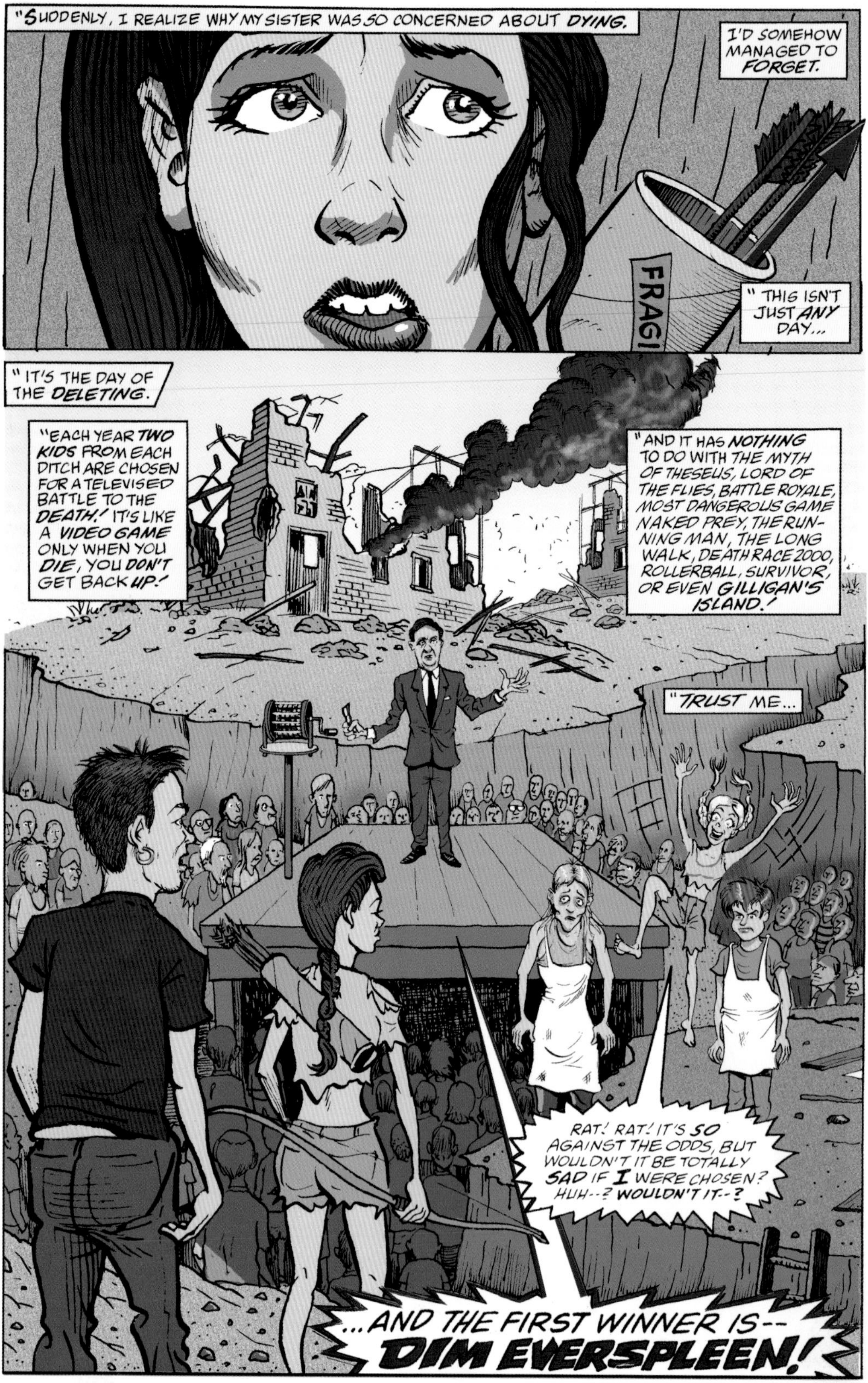
"SUDDENLY, I REALIZE WHY MY SISTER WAS SO CONCERNED ABOUT DYING.
I'D SOMEHOW MANAGED TO FORGET.
FRAGI
"THIS ISN'T JUST ANY DAY...
"IT'S THE DAY OF THE DELETING.
"EACH YEAR TWO KIDS FROM EACH DITCH ARE CHOSEN FOR A TELEVISED BATTLE TO THE DEATH! IT'S LIKE A VIDEO GAME ONLY WHEN YOU DIE, YOU DON'T GET BACK UP!
"AND IT HAS NOTHING TO DO WITH THE MYTH OF THESEUS, LORD OF THE FLIES, BATTLE ROYALE, MOST DANGEROUS GAME NAKED PREY, THE RUNNING MAN, THE LONG WALK, DEATH RACE 2000, ROLLERBALL, SURVIVOR, OR EVEN GILLIGAN'S ISLAND!
"TRUST ME...
RAT! RAT! IT'S SO AGAINST THE ODDS, BUT WOULDN'T IT BE TOTALLY SAD IF I WERE CHOSEN? HUH--? WOULDN'T IT--?
...AND THE FIRST WINNER IS-- DIM EVERSPLEEN!

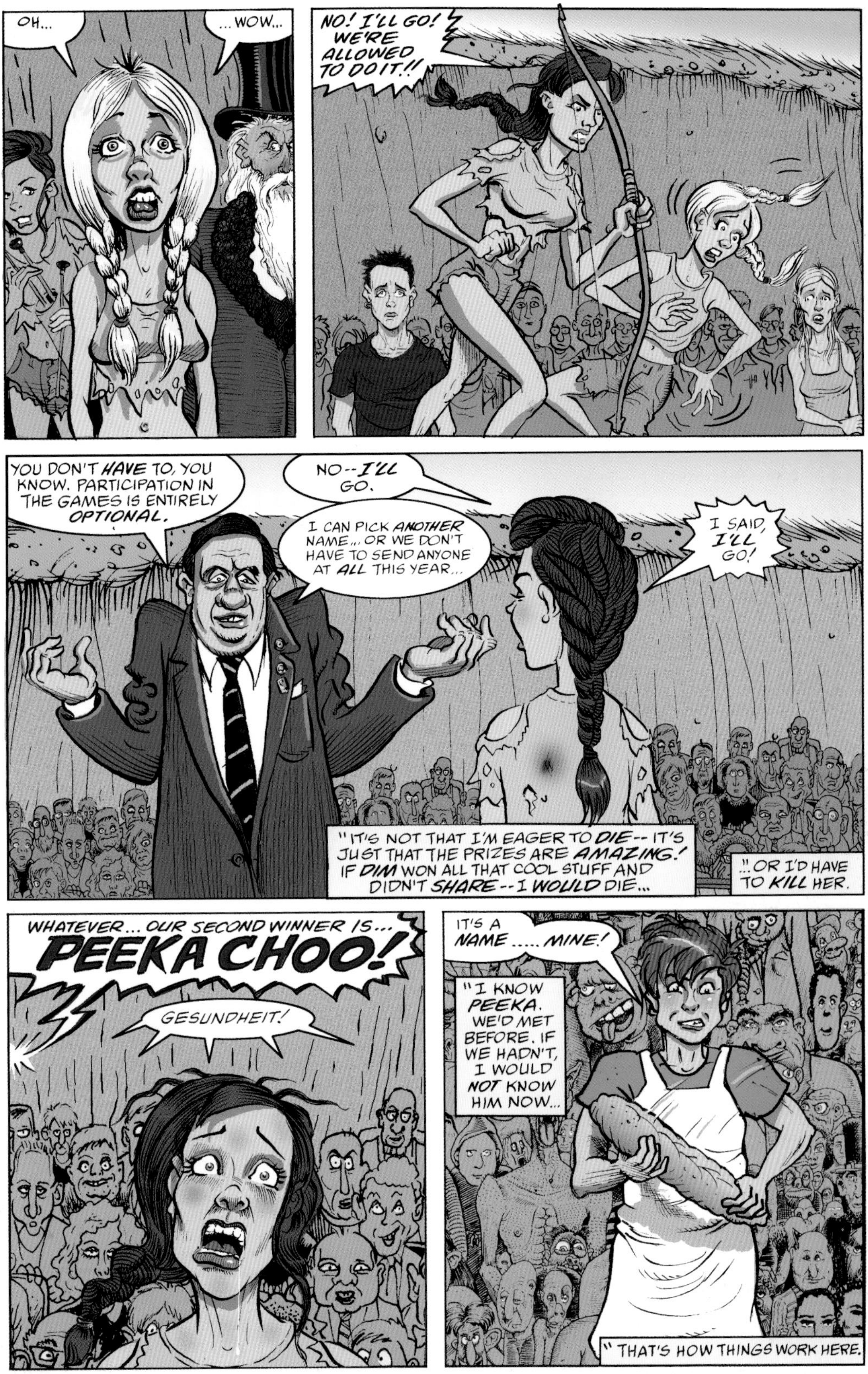
OH...
...WOW...
NO! I'LL GO! WE'RE ALLOWED TO DO IT!!
YOU DON'T HAVE TO, YOU KNOW. PARTICIPATION IN THE GAMES IS ENTIRELY OPTIONAL.
NO--I'LL GO.
I CAN PICK ANOTHER NAME... OR WE DON'T HAVE TO SEND ANYONE AT ALL THIS YEAR...
I SAID, I'LL GO!
"IT'S NOT THAT I'M EAGER TO DIE-- IT'S JUST THAT THE PRIZES ARE AMAZING! IF DIM WON ALL THAT COOL STUFF AND DIDN'T SHARE--I WOULD DIE...
...OR I'D HAVE TO KILL HER.
WHATEVER... OUR SECOND WINNER IS... PEEKA CHOO!
GESUNDHEIT!
IT'S A NAME ..... MINE!
"I KNOW PEEKA. WE'D MET BEFORE. IF WE HADN'T, I WOULD NOT KNOW HIM NOW...
"THAT'S HOW THINGS WORK HERE.

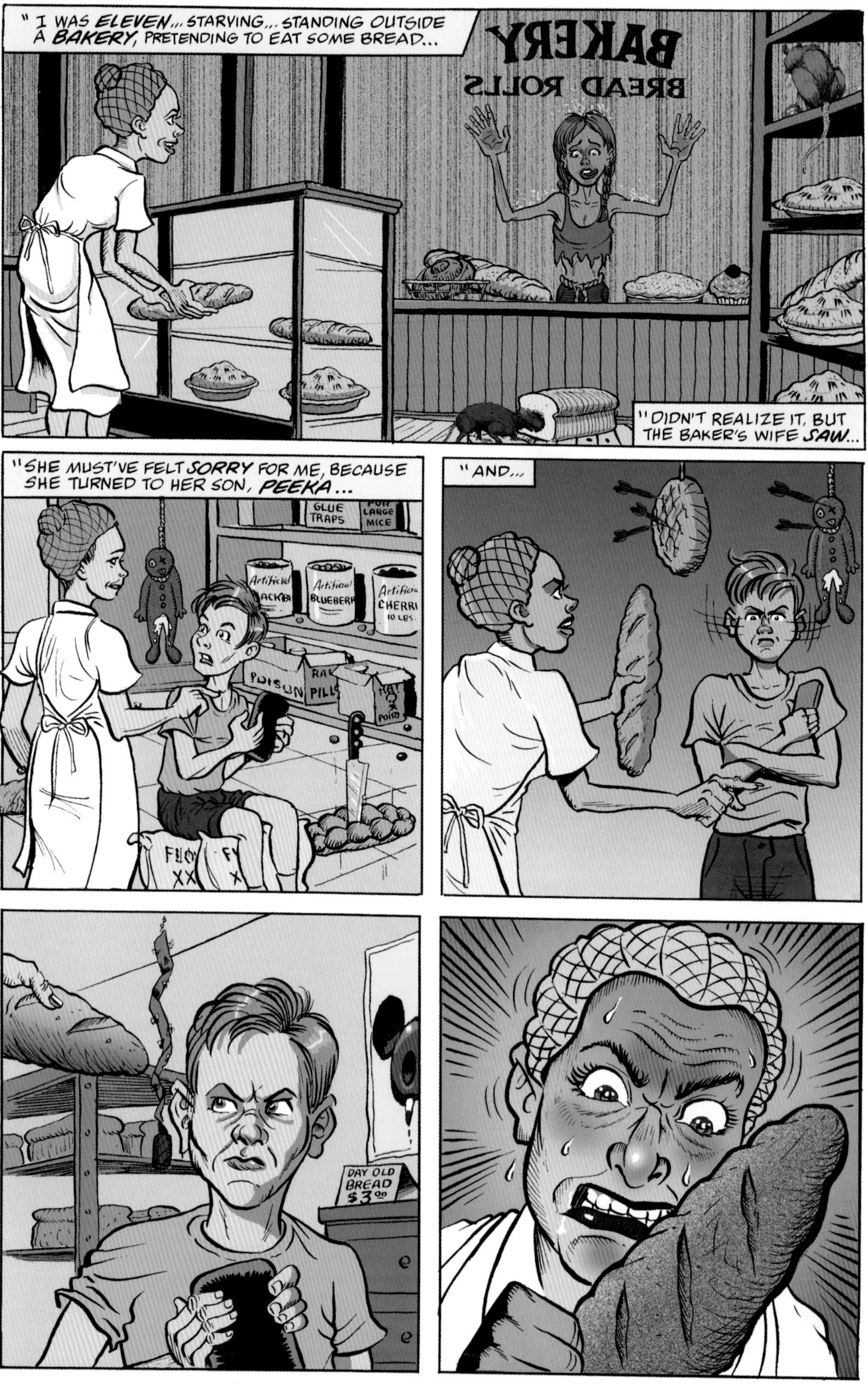

"I WAS ELEVEN... STARVING... STANDING OUTSIDE A BAKERY, PRETENDING TO EAT SOME BREAD...
BAKERY
BREAD ROLLS
"DIDN'T REALIZE IT, BUT THE BAKER'S WIFE SAW...
"SHE MUST'VE FELT SORRY FOR ME, BECAUSE SHE TURNED TO HER SON, PEEKA...
GLUE TRAPS
FOR LARGE MICE
Artificial BLUEBERR
Artificia CHERRI 10 LBS.
POISON
"AND...
DAY OLD BREAD $3.00

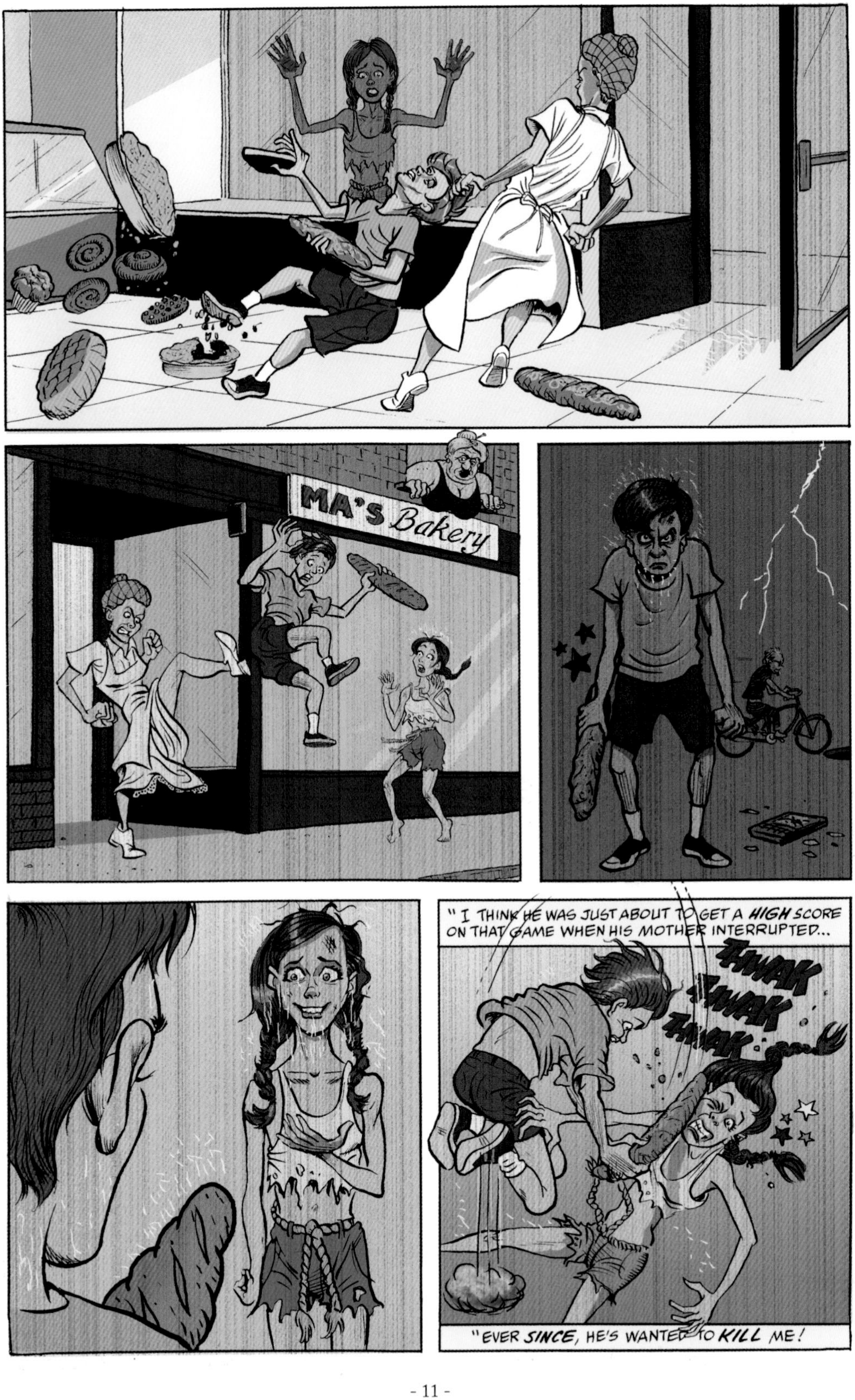
MA'S Bakery
"I THINK HE WAS JUST ABOUT TO GET A HIGH SCORE ON THAT GAME WHEN HIS MOTHER INTERRUPTED...
THWAK
THWAK
THWAK
"EVER SINCE, HE'S WANTED TO KILL ME!

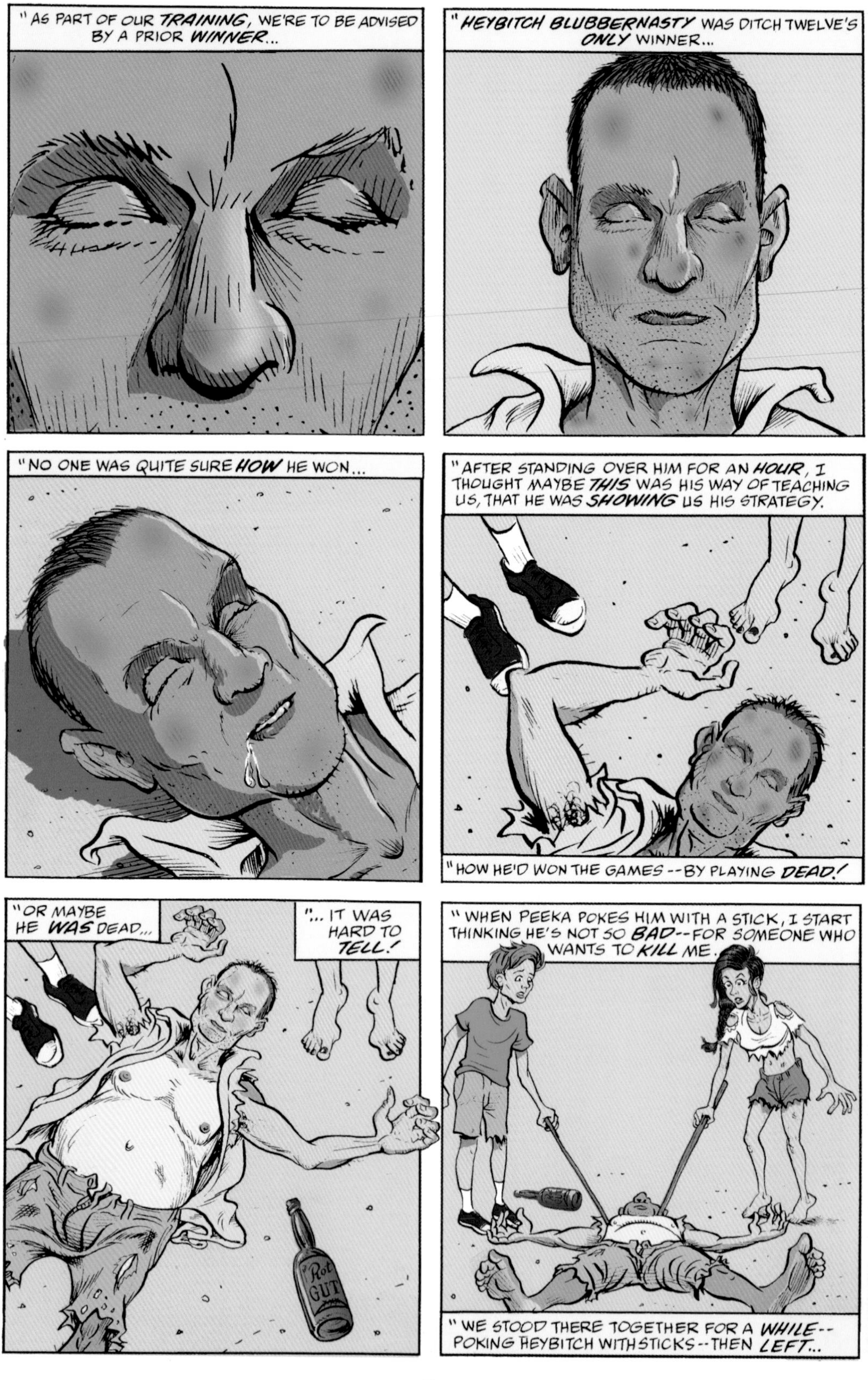
"AS PART OF OUR TRAINING, WE'RE TO BE ADVISED BY A PRIOR WINNER...
"HEYBITCH BLUBBERNASTY WAS DITCH TWELVE'S ONLY WINNER...
"NO ONE WAS QUITE SURE HOW HE WON...
"AFTER STANDING OVER HIM FOR AN HOUR, I THOUGHT MAYBE THIS WAS HIS WAY OF TEACHING US, THAT HE WAS SHOWING US HIS STRATEGY.
"HOW HE'D WON THE GAMES --BY PLAYING DEAD!
"OR MAYBE HE WAS DEAD...
"... IT WAS HARD TO TELL!
Rot GUT
"WHEN PEEKA POKES HIM WITH A STICK, I START THINKING HE'S NOT SO BAD--FOR SOMEONE WHO WANTS TO KILL ME.
"WE STOOD THERE TOGETHER FOR A WHILE-- POKING HEYBITCH WITH STICKS--THEN LEFT...

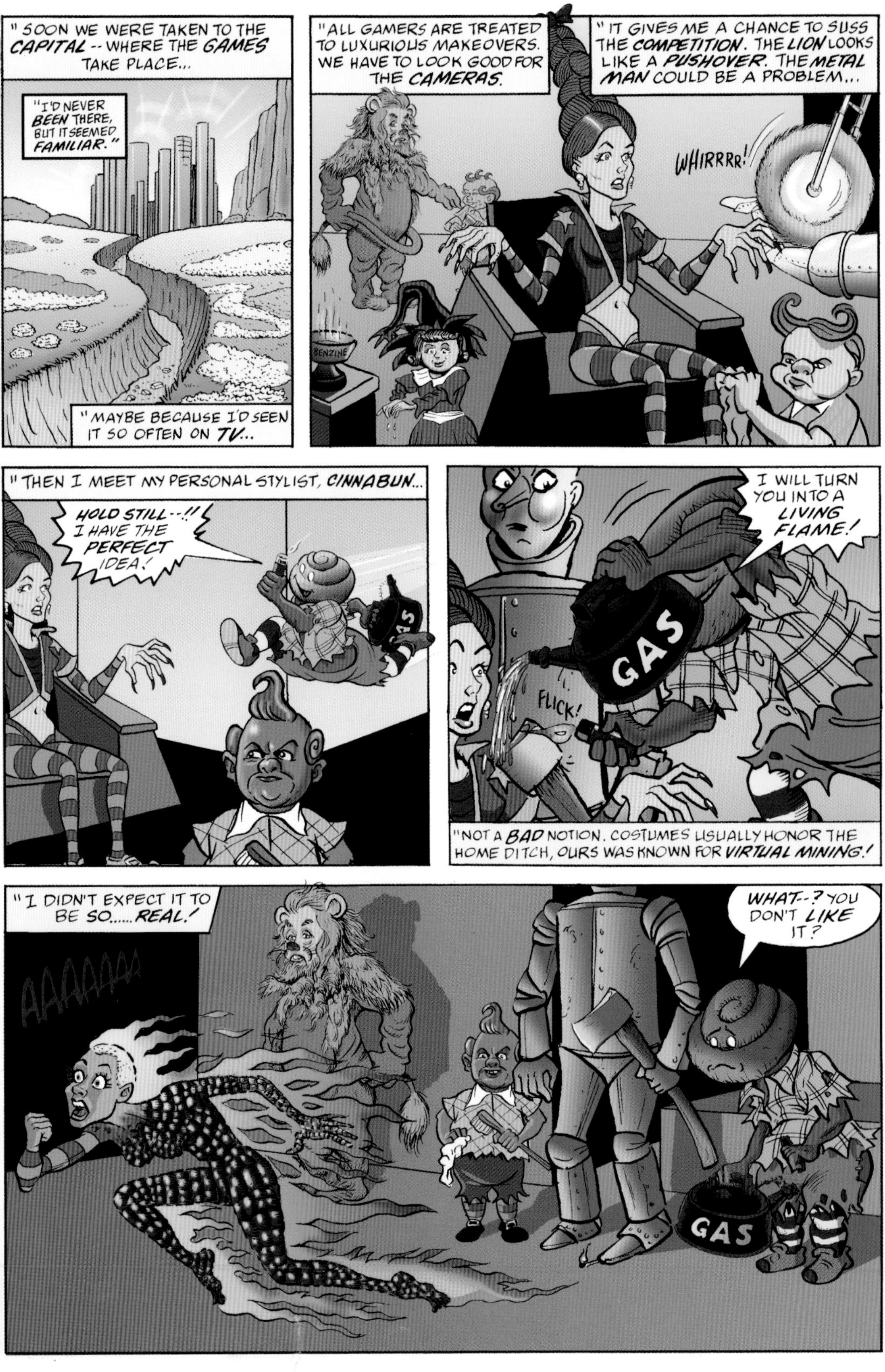
"SOON WE WERE TAKEN TO THE CAPITAL -- WHERE THE GAMES TAKE PLACE...
"I'D NEVER BEEN THERE, BUT IT SEEMED FAMILIAR."
"MAYBE BECAUSE I'D SEEN IT SO OFTEN ON TV...
"ALL GAMERS ARE TREATED TO LUXURIOUS MAKEOVERS. WE HAVE TO LOOK GOOD FOR THE CAMERAS.
"IT GIVES ME A CHANCE TO SUSS THE COMPETITION. THE LION LOOKS LIKE A PUSHOVER. THE METAL MAN COULD BE A PROBLEM...
WHIRRRR!
BENZINE
"THEN I MEET MY PERSONAL STYLIST, CINNABUN...
HOLD STILL--!! I HAVE THE PERFECT IDEA!
I WILL TURN YOU INTO A LIVING FLAME!
GAS
FLICK!
"NOT A BAD NOTION. COSTUMES USUALLY HONOR THE HOME DITCH, OURS WAS KNOWN FOR VIRTUAL MINING!
"I DIDN'T EXPECT IT TO BE SO...... REAL!
AAAAAAA
WHAT--? YOU DON'T LIKE IT?
GAS

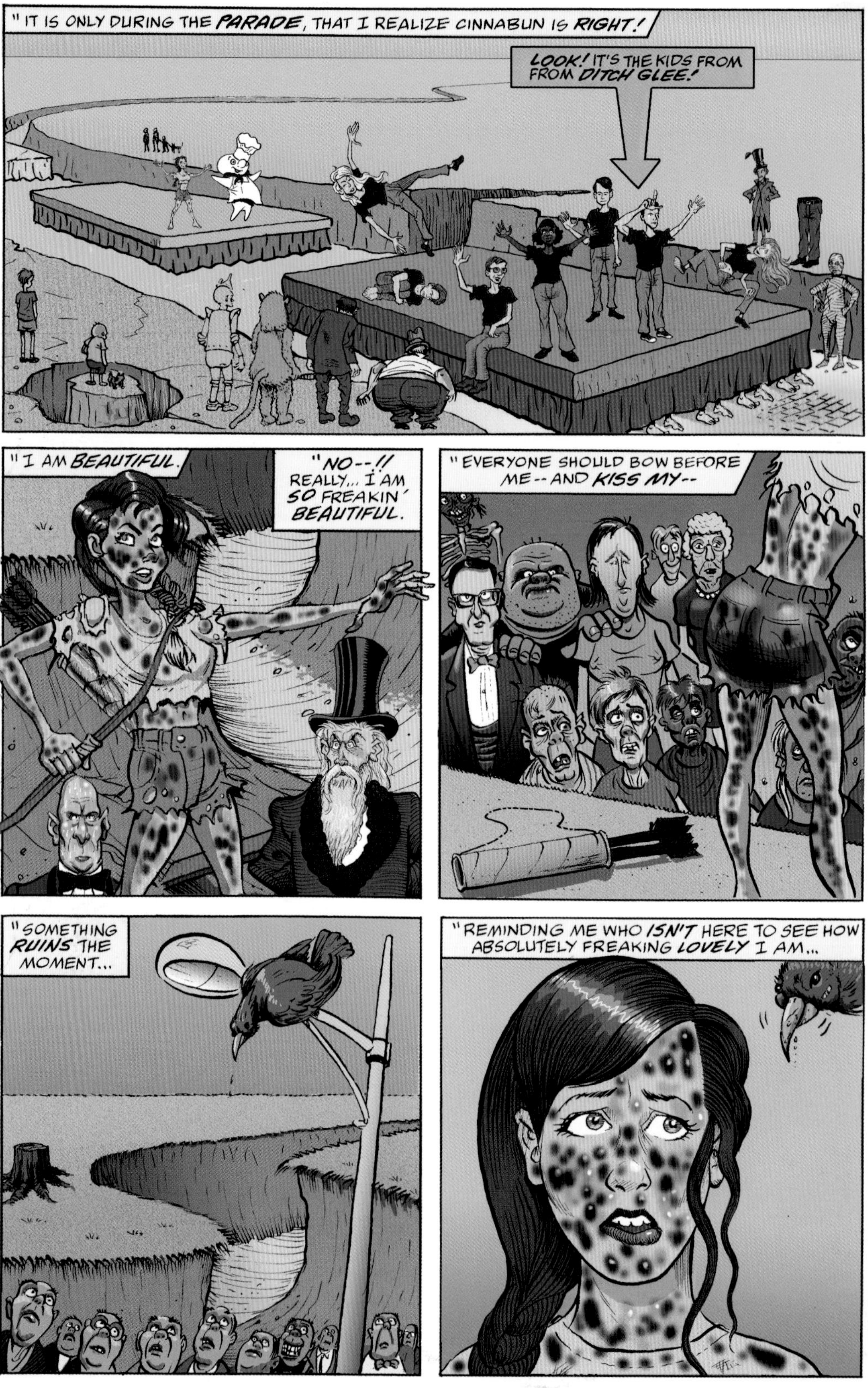
"IT IS ONLY DURING THE PARADE, THAT I REALIZE CINNABUN IS RIGHT!
LOOK! IT'S THE KIDS FROM FROM DITCH GLEE!
"I AM BEAUTIFUL.
"NO--!! REALLY... I AM SO FREAKIN' BEAUTIFUL.
"EVERYONE SHOULD BOW BEFORE ME--AND KISS MY--
"SOMETHING RUINS THE MOMENT...
"REMINDING ME WHO ISN'T HERE TO SEE HOW ABSOLUTELY FREAKING LOVELY I AM...

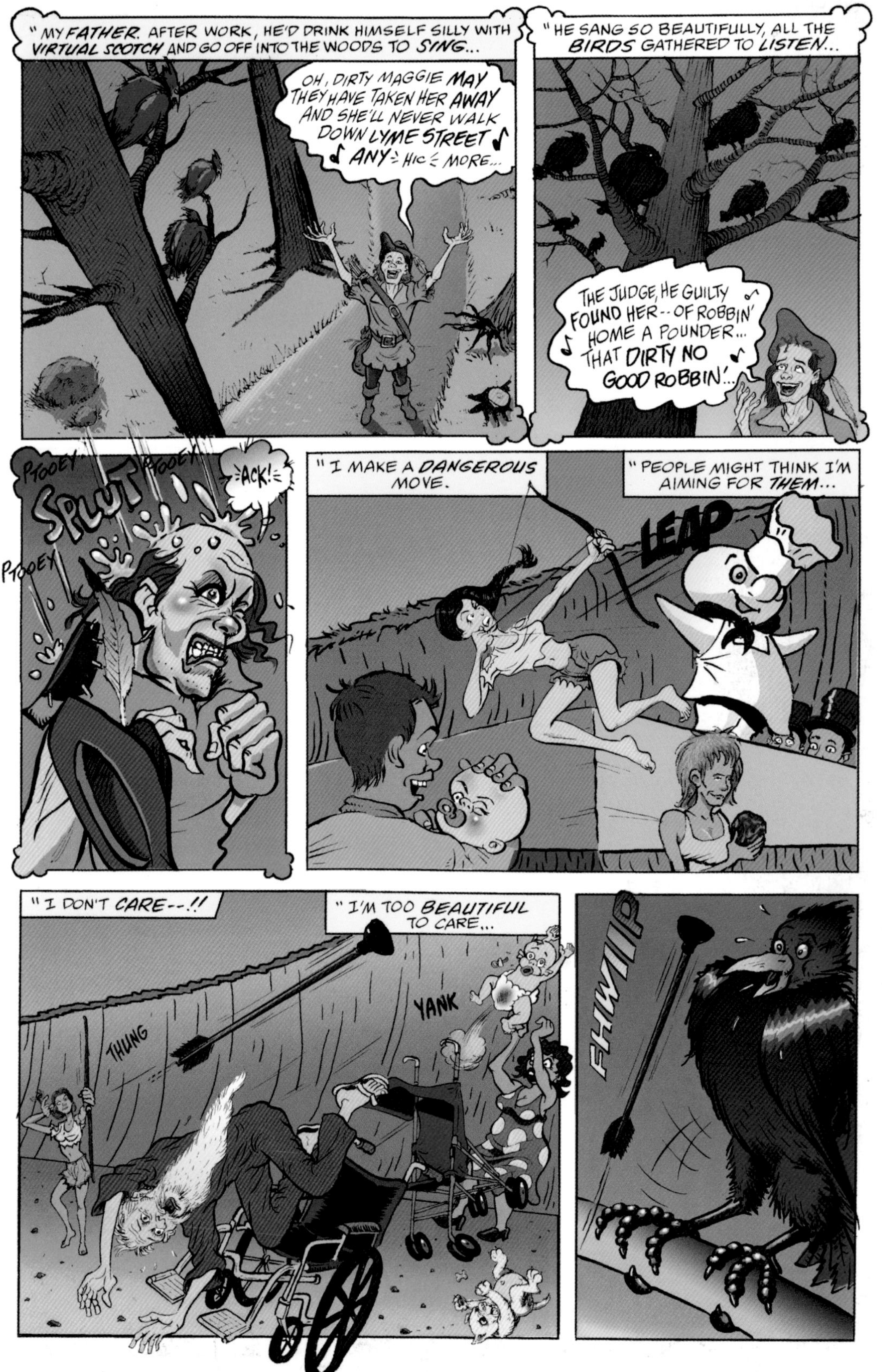
"MY FATHER. AFTER WORK, HE'D DRINK HIMSELF SILLY WITH VIRTUAL SCOTCH AND GO OFF INTO THE WOODS TO SING...
OH, DIRTY MAGGIE MAY THEY HAVE TAKEN HER AWAY AND SHE'LL NEVER WALK DOWN LYME STREET ANY - HIC - MORE...
"HE SANG SO BEAUTIFULLY, ALL THE BIRDS GATHERED TO LISTEN...
THE JUDGE, HE GUILTY FOUND HER -- OF ROBBIN' HOME A POUNDER... THAT DIRTY NO GOOD ROBBIN'...
PTOOEY
SPLUT
PTOOEY
ACK!
PTOOEY
"I MAKE A DANGEROUS MOVE.
"PEOPLE MIGHT THINK I'M AIMING FOR THEM...
LEAP
"I DON'T CARE--!!
"I'M TOO BEAUTIFUL TO CARE...
THUNG
YANK
FHWIIIP

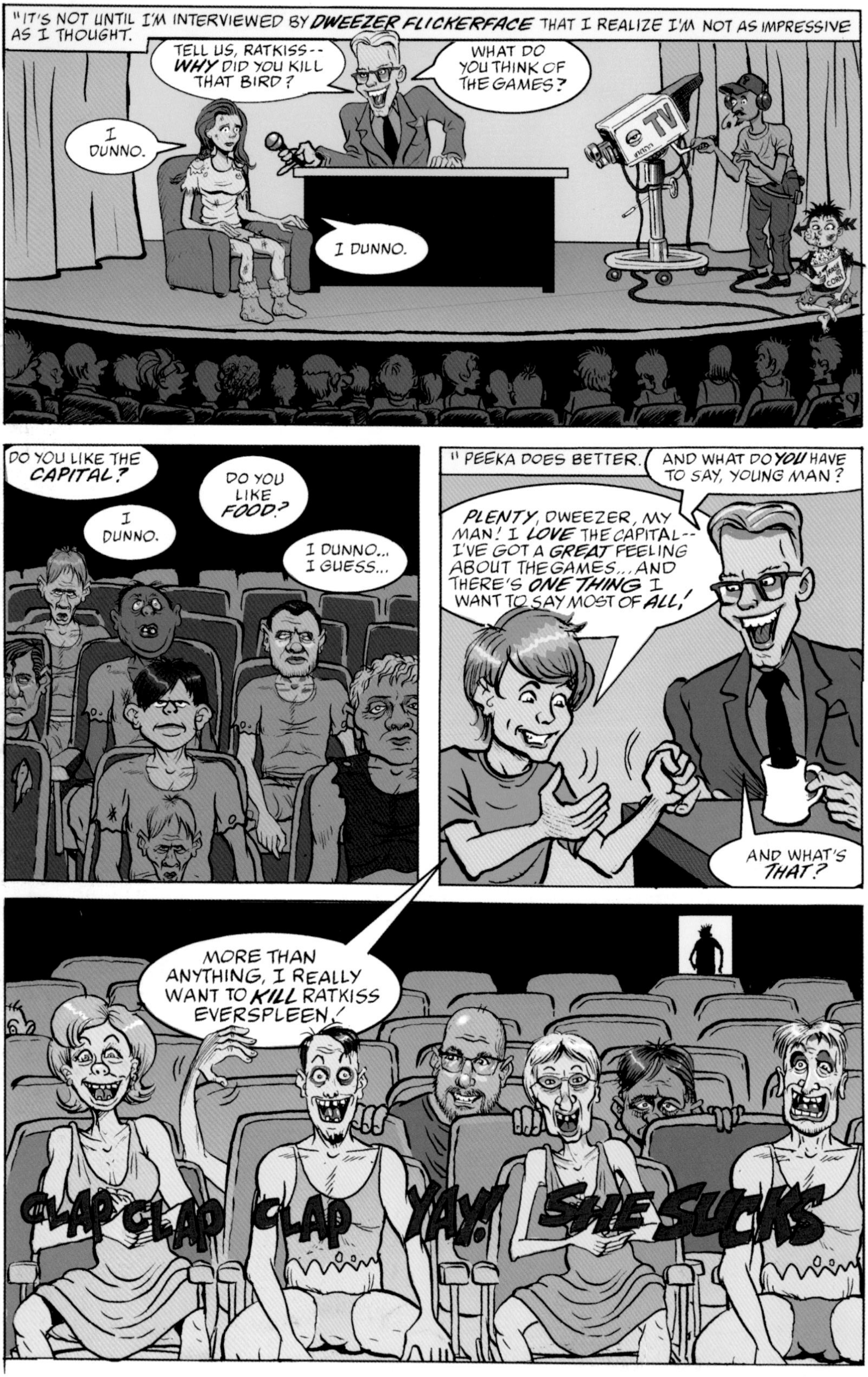
"IT'S NOT UNTIL I'M INTERVIEWED BY DWEEZER FLICKERFACE THAT I REALIZE I'M NOT AS IMPRESSIVE AS I THOUGHT.
TELL US, RATKISS-- WHY DID YOU KILL THAT BIRD?
I DUNNO.
WHAT DO YOU THINK OF THE GAMES?
I DUNNO.
TV
DO YOU LIKE THE CAPITAL?
I DUNNO.
DO YOU LIKE FOOD?
I DUNNO... I GUESS...
" PEEKA DOES BETTER.
AND WHAT DO YOU HAVE TO SAY, YOUNG MAN?
PLENTY, DWEEZER, MY MAN! I LOVE THE CAPITAL-- I'VE GOT A GREAT FEELING ABOUT THE GAMES... AND THERE'S ONE THING I WANT TO SAY MOST OF ALL!
AND WHAT'S THAT?
MORE THAN ANYTHING, I REALLY WANT TO KILL RATKISS EVERSPLEEN!
CLAP CLAP CLAP YAY! SHE SUCKS

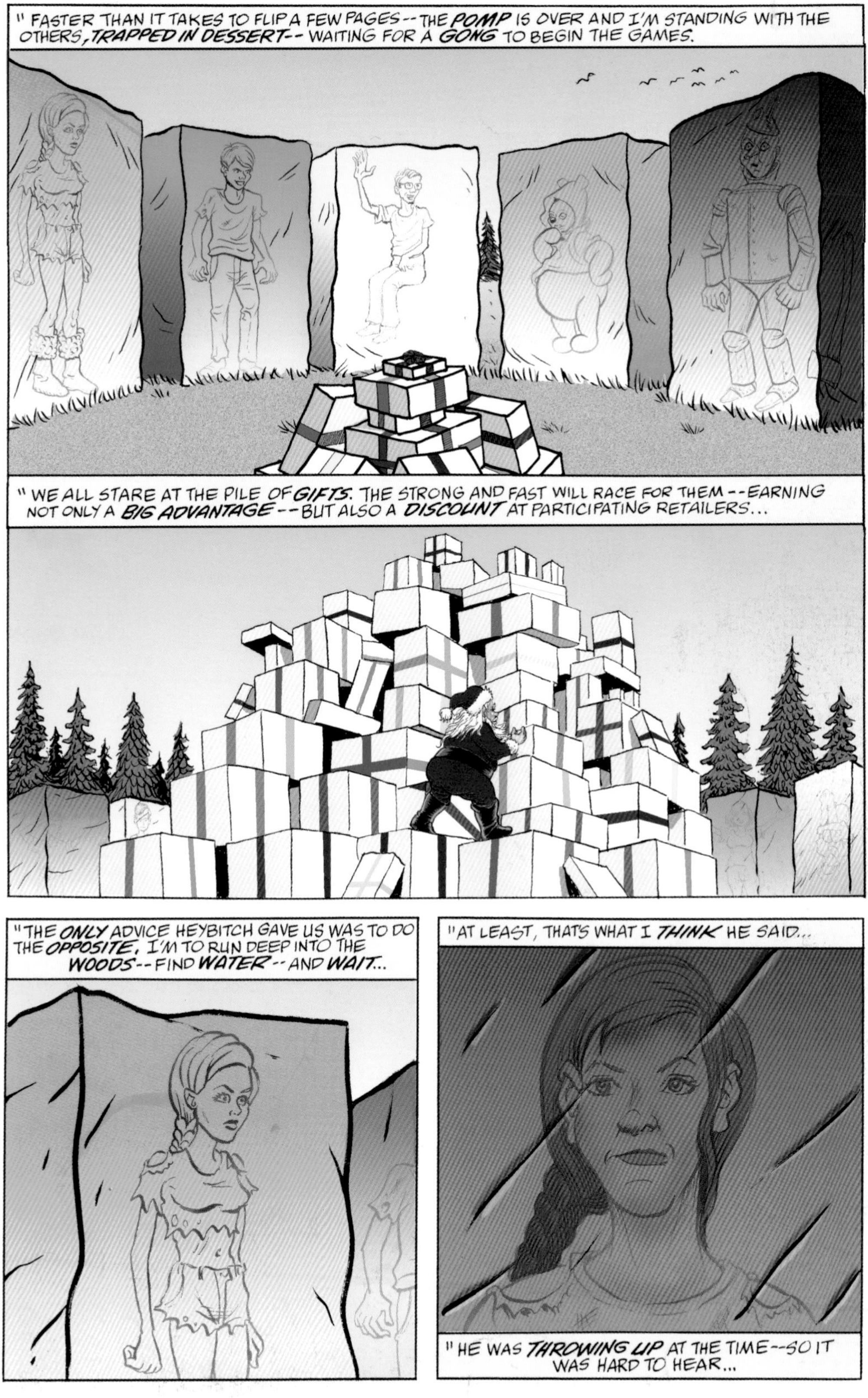
" FASTER THAN IT TAKES TO FLIP A FEW PAGES -- THE POMP IS OVER AND I'M STANDING WITH THE OTHERS, TRAPPED IN DESSERT-- WAITING FOR A GONG TO BEGIN THE GAMES.
" WE ALL STARE AT THE PILE OF GIFTS. THE STRONG AND FAST WILL RACE FOR THEM -- EARNING NOT ONLY A BIG ADVANTAGE -- BUT ALSO A DISCOUNT AT PARTICIPATING RETAILERS...
"THE ONLY ADVICE HEYBITCH GAVE US WAS TO DO THE OPPOSITE. I'M TO RUN DEEP INTO THE WOODS -- FIND WATER -- AND WAIT...
"AT LEAST, THAT'S WHAT I THINK HE SAID...
" HE WAS THROWING UP AT THE TIME -- SO IT WAS HARD TO HEAR...

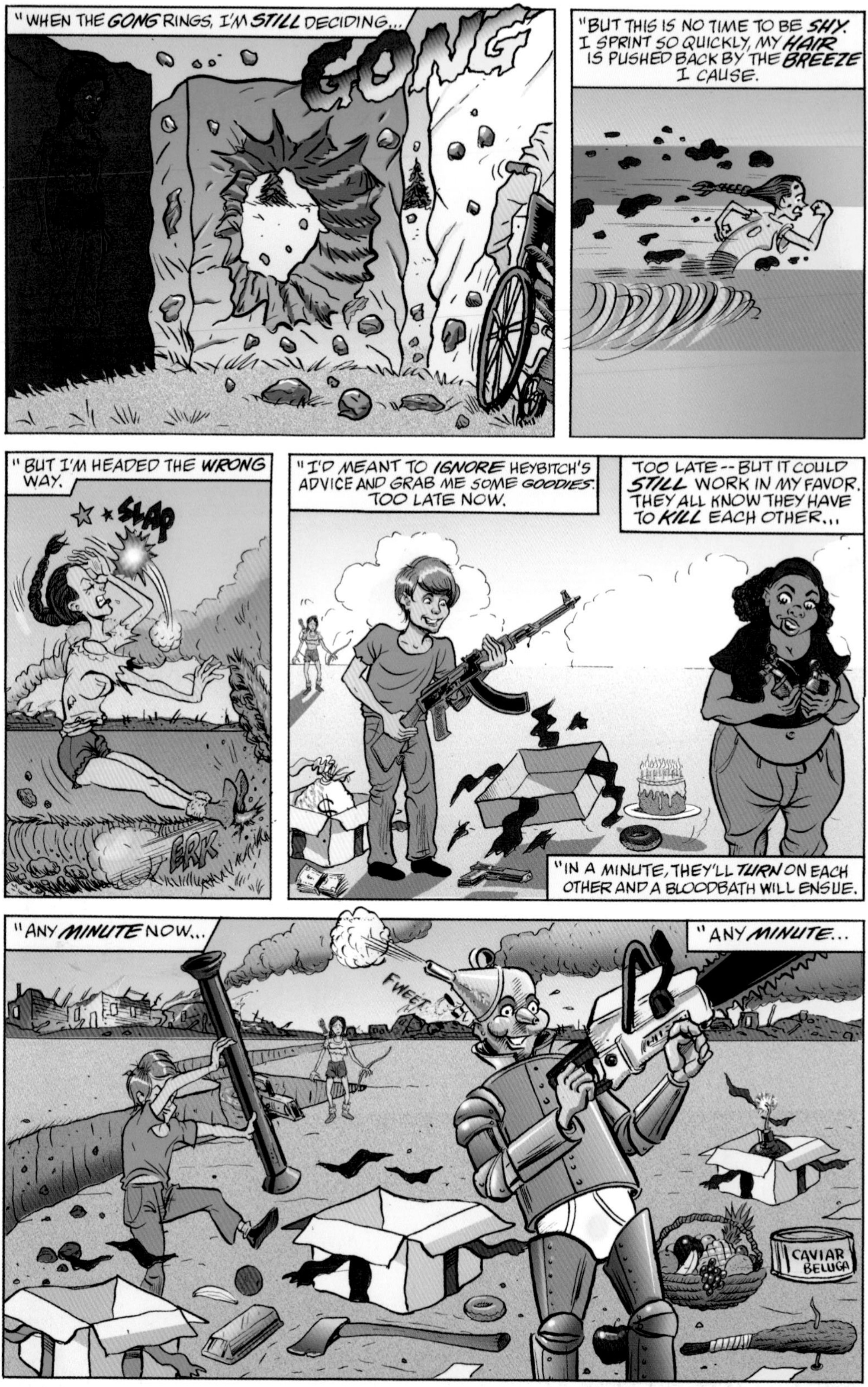
"WHEN THE GONG RINGS, I'M STILL DECIDING...
GONG
"BUT THIS IS NO TIME TO BE SHY. I SPRINT SO QUICKLY, MY HAIR IS PUSHED BACK BY THE BREEZE I CAUSE.
"BUT I'M HEADED THE WRONG WAY.
SLAP
ERK
"I'D MEANT TO IGNORE HEYBITCH'S ADVICE AND GRAB ME SOME GOODIES. TOO LATE NOW.
TOO LATE -- BUT IT COULD STILL WORK IN MY FAVOR. THEY ALL KNOW THEY HAVE TO KILL EACH OTHER...
"IN A MINUTE, THEY'LL TURN ON EACH OTHER AND A BLOODBATH WILL ENSUE.
"ANY MINUTE NOW...
"ANY MINUTE...
FWEET
CAVIAR BELUGA

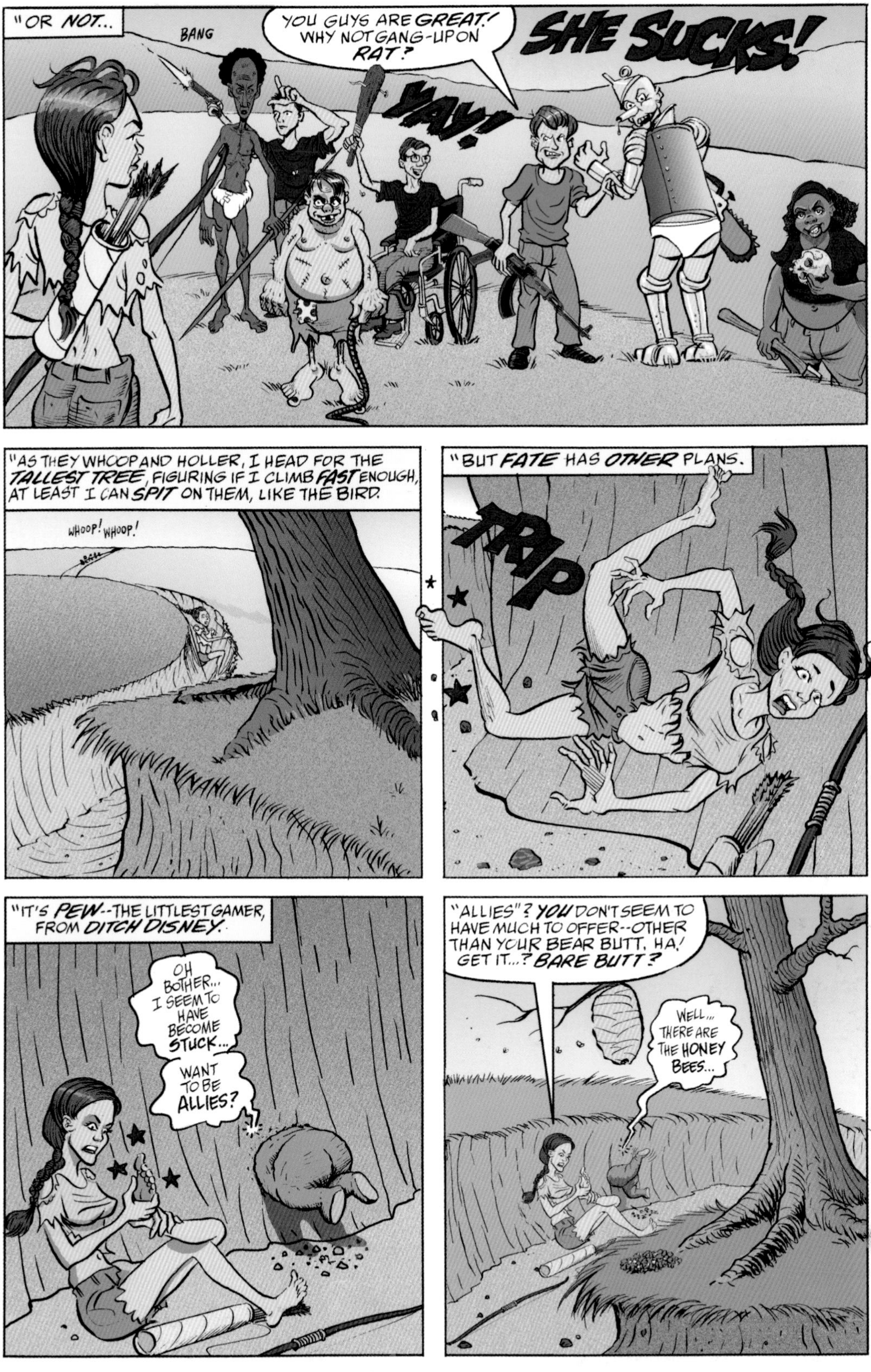
"OR NOT...
BANG
YOU GUYS ARE GREAT! WHY NOT GANG-UP ON RAT?
SHE SUCKS!
YAY!
"AS THEY WHOOP AND HOLLER, I HEAD FOR THE TALLEST TREE, FIGURING IF I CLIMB FAST ENOUGH, AT LEAST I CAN SPIT ON THEM, LIKE THE BIRD.
WHOOP! WHOOP!
"BUT FATE HAS OTHER PLANS.
TRAP
"IT'S PEW--THE LITTLEST GAMER, FROM DITCH DISNEY.
OH BOTHER... I SEEM TO HAVE BECOME STUCK...
WANT TO BE ALLIES?
"ALLIES"? YOU DON'T SEEM TO HAVE MUCH TO OFFER--OTHER THAN YOUR BEAR BUTT, HA! GET IT...? BARE BUTT?
WELL... THERE ARE THE HONEY BEES...

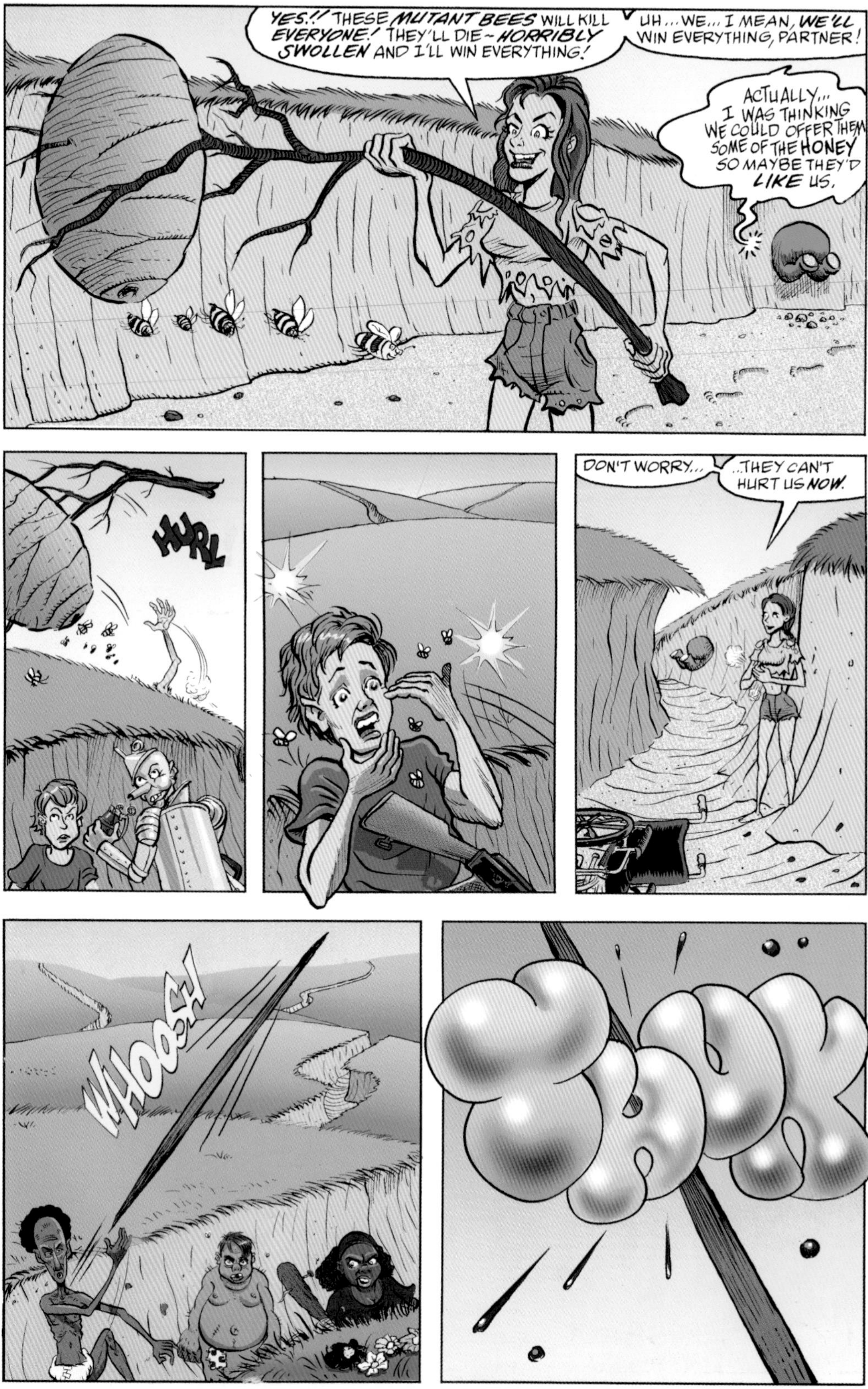
YES!! THESE MUTANT BEES WILL KILL EVERYONE! THEY'LL DIE~HORRIBLY SWOLLEN AND I'LL WIN EVERYTHING!
UH... WE... I MEAN, WE'LL WIN EVERYTHING, PARTNER!
ACTUALLY... I WAS THINKING WE COULD OFFER THEM SOME OF THE HONEY SO MAYBE THEY'D LIKE US.
HURL
DON'T WORRY...
...THEY CAN'T HURT US NOW.
WHOOSH

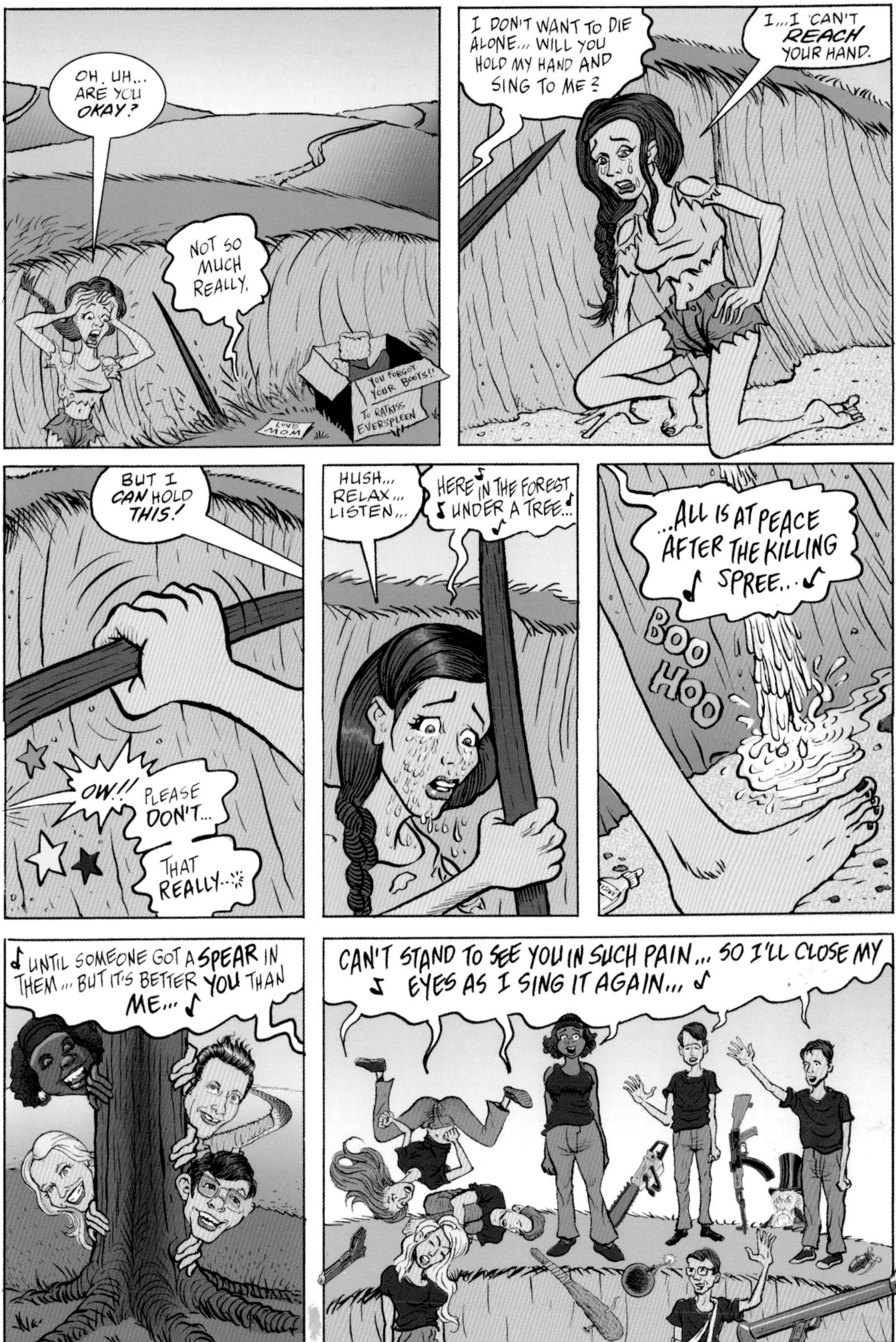
OH, UH... ARE YOU OKAY?
NOT SO MUCH REALLY.
YOU FORGOT YOUR BOOTS!!
TO RATKISS EVERSPLEEN
LOVE MOM
I DON'T WANT TO DIE ALONE... WILL YOU HOLD MY HAND AND SING TO ME?
I...I CAN'T REACH YOUR HAND.
BUT I CAN HOLD THIS!
OW!!
PLEASE DON'T...
THAT REALLY...
HUSH... RELAX... LISTEN...
HERE IN THE FOREST UNDER A TREE...
...ALL IS AT PEACE AFTER THE KILLING SPREE...
BOO HOO
UNTIL SOMEONE GOT A SPEAR IN THEM... BUT IT'S BETTER YOU THAN ME...
DANNY
"BUT WE'RE NOT ALONE!
CAN'T STAND TO SEE YOU IN SUCH PAIN... SO I'LL CLOSE MY EYES AS I SING IT AGAIN...
"I'M SHOCKED. THE KIDS FROM DITCH GLEE ARE SO MOVED THEY'VE COME TO SHARE THE MOMENT.
"SOMEHOW DESPITE EVERYTHING...

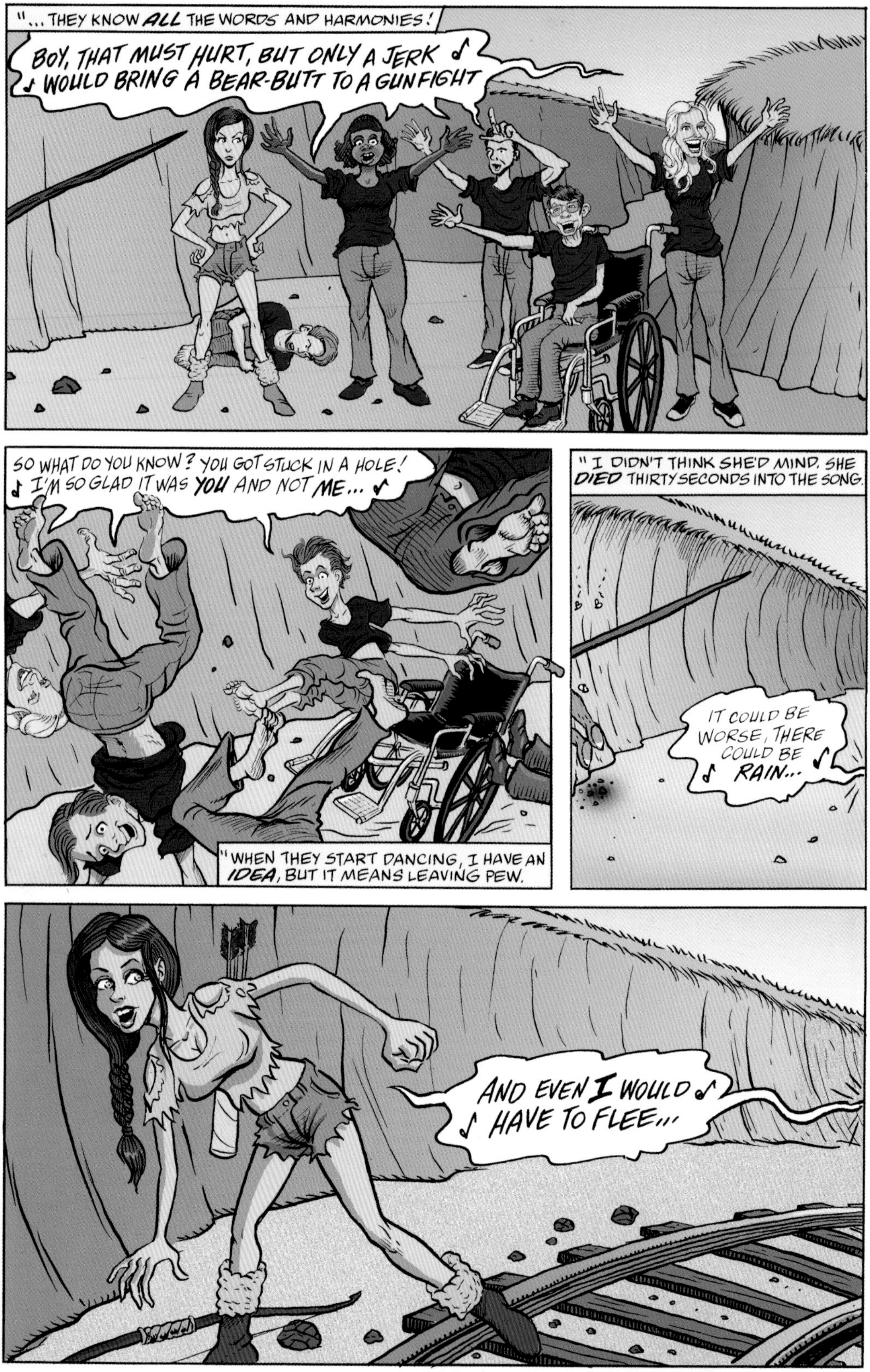
"... THEY KNOW ALL THE WORDS AND HARMONIES!
BOY, THAT MUST HURT, BUT ONLY A JERK ♪ ♪ WOULD BRING A BEAR-BUTT TO A GUNFIGHT
SO WHAT DO YOU KNOW? YOU GOT STUCK IN A HOLE! ♪ I'M SO GLAD IT WAS YOU AND NOT ME... ♪
"WHEN THEY START DANCING, I HAVE AN IDEA, BUT IT MEANS LEAVING PEW.
"I DIDN'T THINK SHE'D MIND. SHE DIED THIRTY SECONDS INTO THE SONG.
IT COULD BE WORSE, THERE COULD BE ♪ RAIN... ♪
AND EVEN I WOULD ♪ ♪ HAVE TO FLEE...

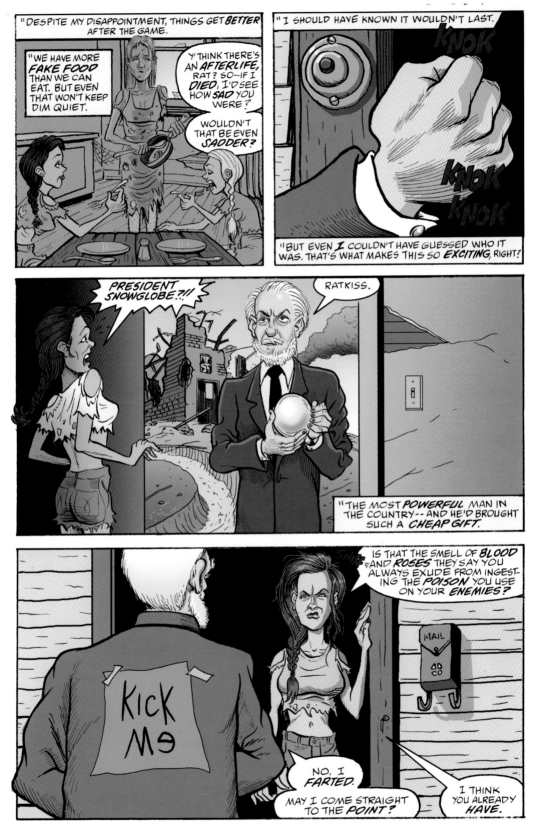

"DESPITE MY DISAPPOINTMENT, THINGS GET *BETTER* AFTER THE GAME.

"WE HAVE MORE *FAKE FOOD* THAN WE CAN EAT. BUT EVEN THAT WON'T KEEP DIM QUIET.

Y' THINK THERE'S AN *AFTERLIFE*, RAT? SO--IF I *DIED*, I'D SEE HOW *SAD* YOU WERE?

WOULDN'T THAT BE EVEN *SADDER*?

"I SHOULD HAVE KNOWN IT WOULDN'T LAST.

KNOK

KNOK

KNOK

"BUT EVEN *I* COULDN'T HAVE GUESSED WHO IT WAS. THAT'S WHAT MAKES THIS SO *EXCITING*, RIGHT?

PRESIDENT SNOWGLOBE?!!

RATKISS.

"THE MOST *POWERFUL* MAN IN THE COUNTRY-- AND HE'D BROUGHT SUCH A *CHEAP GIFT*.

IS THAT THE SMELL OF *BLOOD* AND *ROSES* THEY SAY YOU ALWAYS EXUDE FROM INGESTING THE *POISON* YOU USE ON YOUR *ENEMIES*?

KICK ME

NO, I *FARTED*.

MAY I COME STRAIGHT TO THE *POINT*?

I THINK YOU ALREADY *HAVE*.

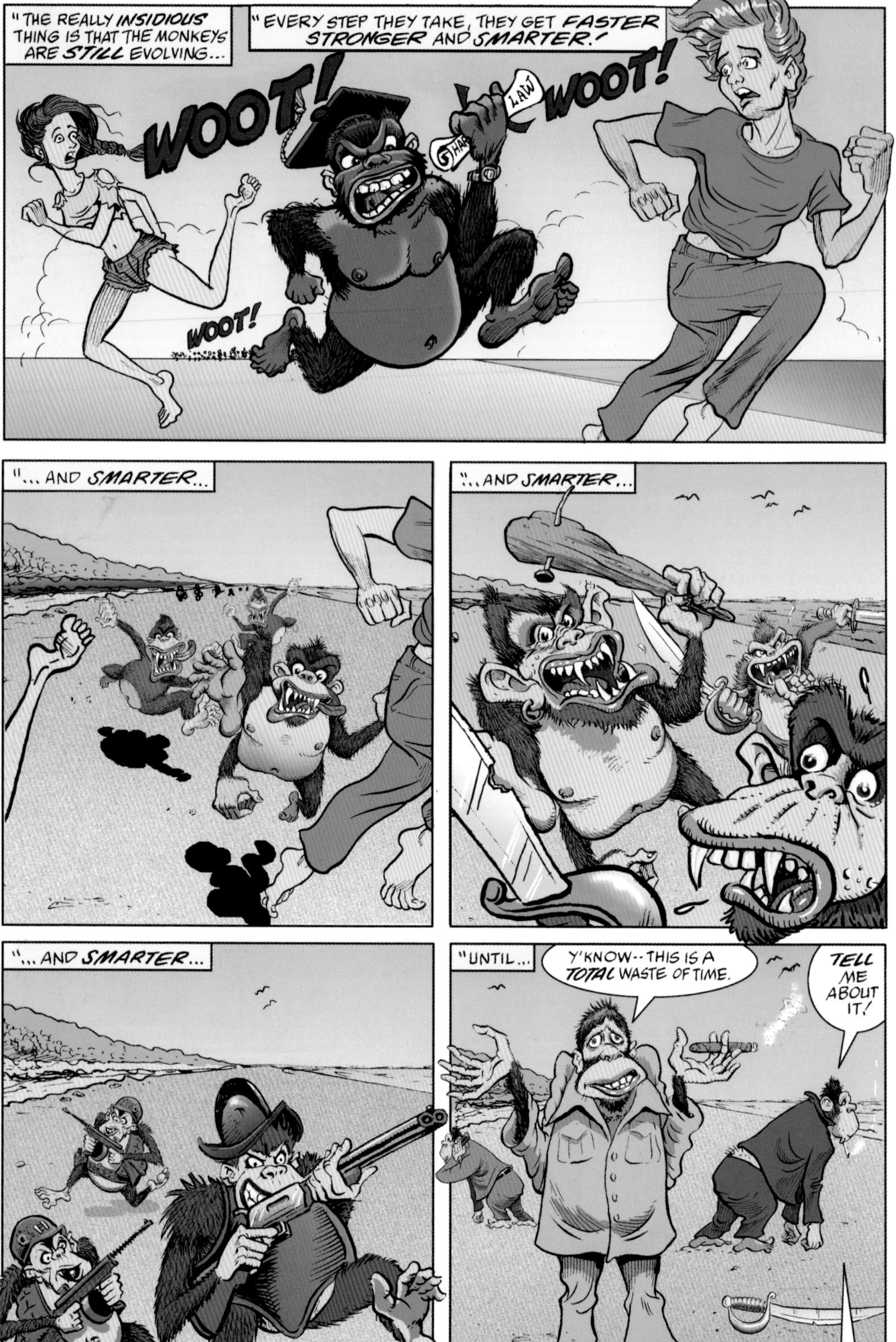
"THE REALLY INSIDIOUS THING IS THAT THE MONKEYS ARE STILL EVOLVING...
"EVERY STEP THEY TAKE, THEY GET FASTER STRONGER AND SMARTER.'
WOOT!
LAW
WOOT!
WOOT!
"... AND SMARTER...
"... AND SMARTER...
"... AND SMARTER...
"UNTIL...
Y'KNOW-- THIS IS A TOTAL WASTE OF TIME.
TELL ME ABOUT IT!
LET'S GET A LATTE.

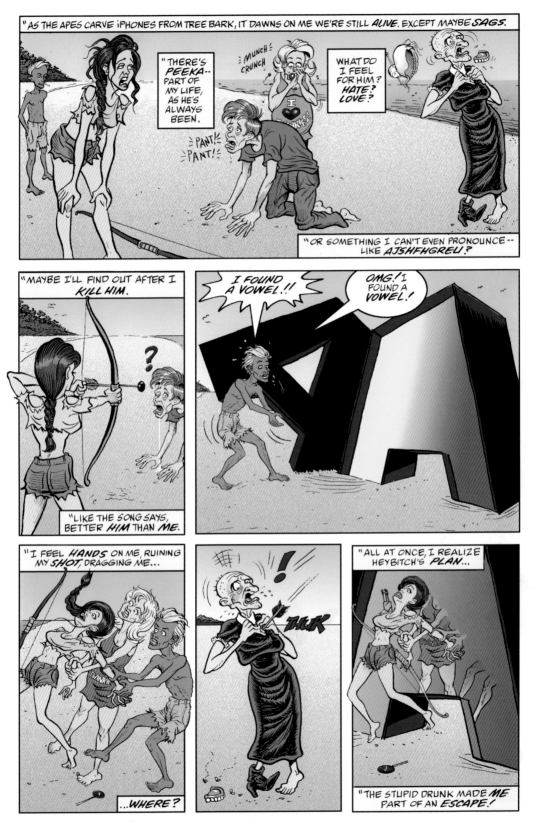

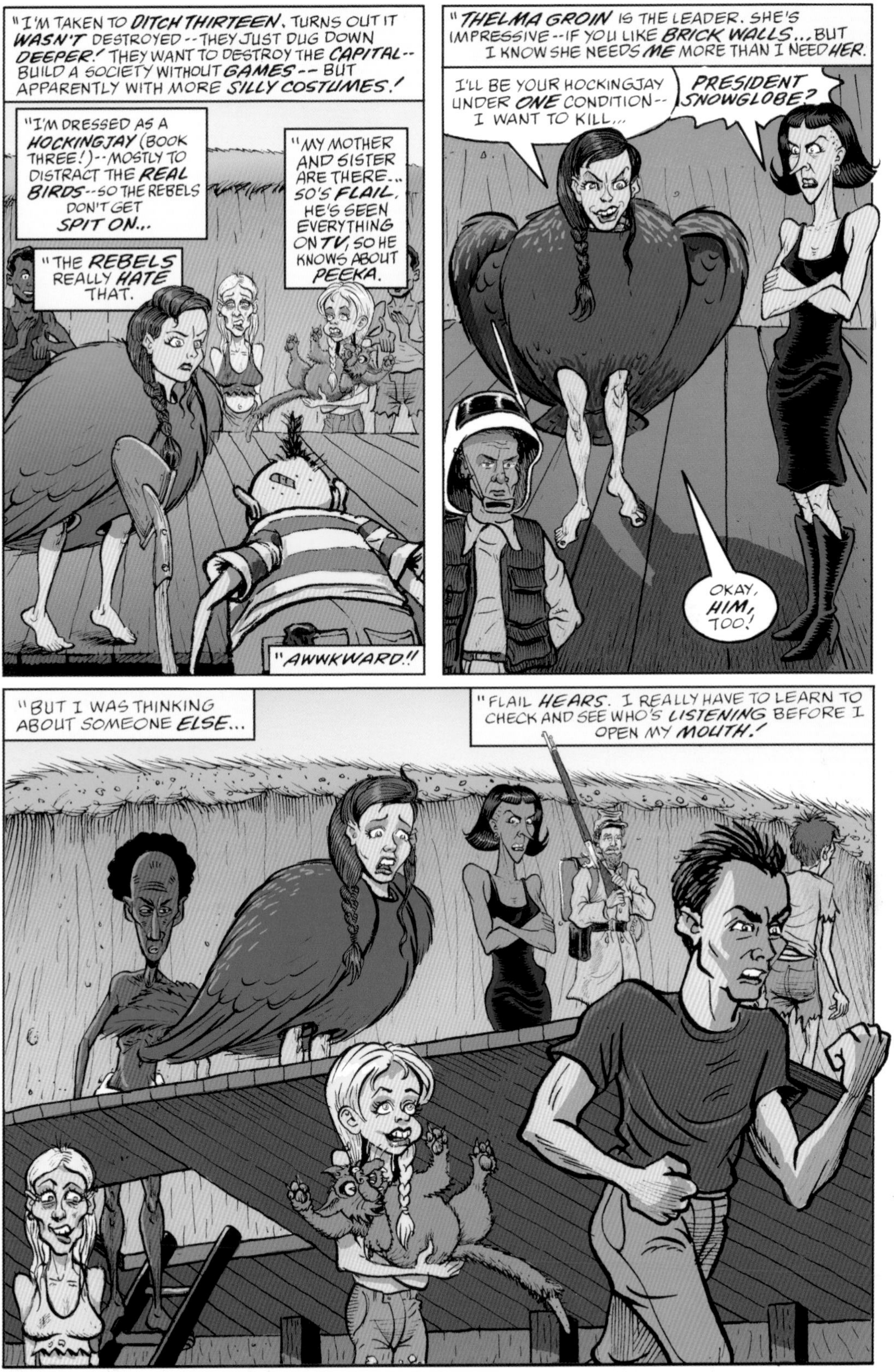

"I'M TAKEN TO DITCH THIRTEEN. TURNS OUT IT WASN'T DESTROYED--THEY JUST DUG DOWN DEEPER! THEY WANT TO DESTROY THE CAPITAL--BUILD A SOCIETY WITHOUT GAMES--BUT APPARENTLY WITH MORE SILLY COSTUMES!
"I'M DRESSED AS A HOCKINGJAY (BOOK THREE!)--MOSTLY TO DISTRACT THE REAL BIRDS--SO THE REBELS DON'T GET SPIT ON...
"MY MOTHER AND SISTER ARE THERE... SO'S FLAIL. HE'S SEEN EVERYTHING ON TV, SO HE KNOWS ABOUT PEEKA.
"THE REBELS REALLY HATE THAT.
"AWWKWARD!!
"THELMA GROIN IS THE LEADER. SHE'S IMPRESSIVE--IF YOU LIKE BRICK WALLS... BUT I KNOW SHE NEEDS ME MORE THAN I NEED HER.
I'LL BE YOUR HOCKINGJAY UNDER ONE CONDITION--I WANT TO KILL...
PRESIDENT SNOWGLOBE?
OKAY, HIM, TOO!
"BUT I WAS THINKING ABOUT SOMEONE ELSE...
"FLAIL HEARS. I REALLY HAVE TO LEARN TO CHECK AND SEE WHO'S LISTENING BEFORE I OPEN MY MOUTH!

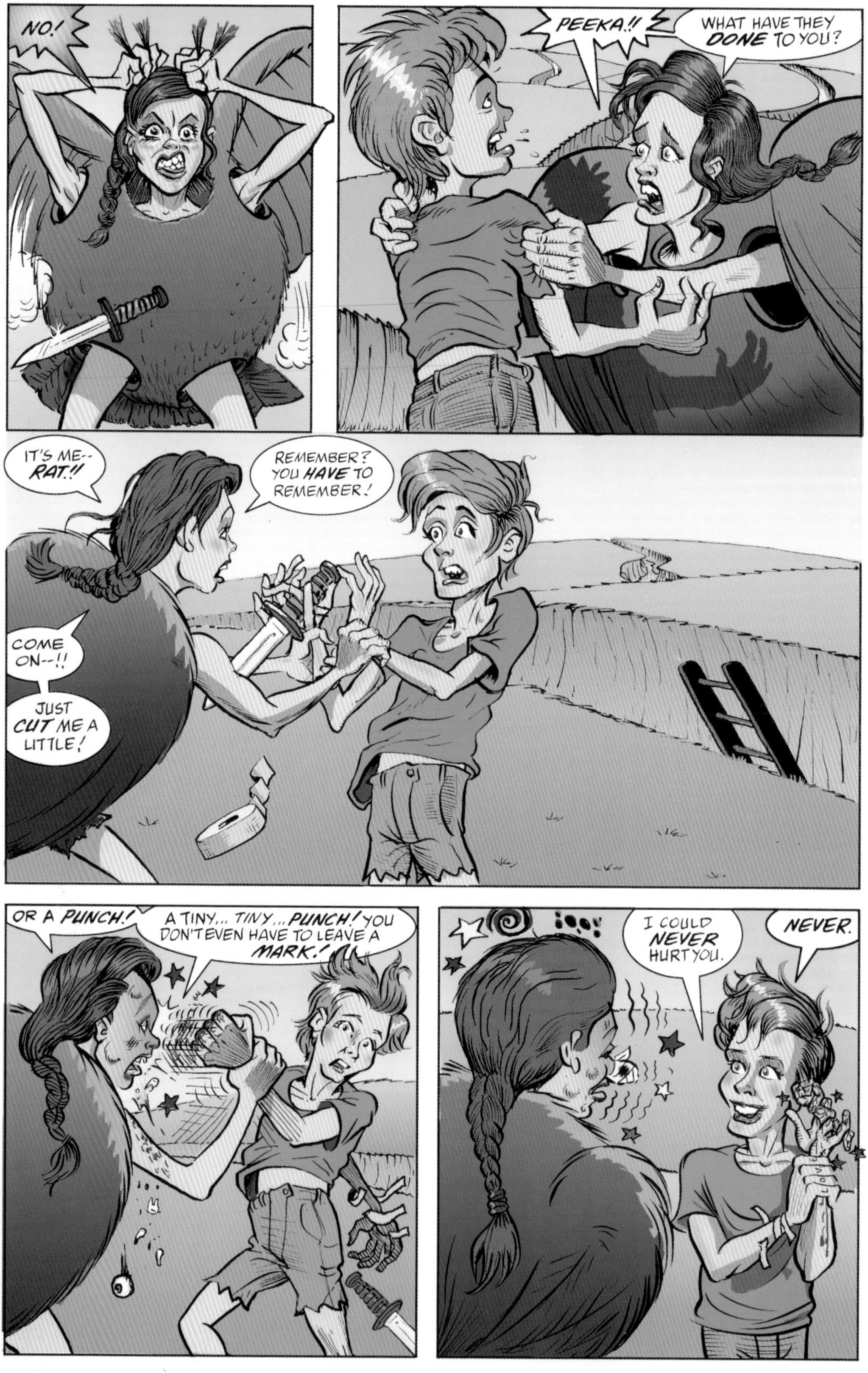
NO!
PEEKA!!
WHAT HAVE THEY DONE TO YOU?
IT'S ME-- RAT!!
REMEMBER? YOU HAVE TO REMEMBER!
COME ON--!!
JUST CUT ME A LITTLE!
OR A PUNCH!
A TINY... TINY... PUNCH! YOU DON'T EVEN HAVE TO LEAVE A MARK!
I COULD NEVER HURT YOU.
NEVER.

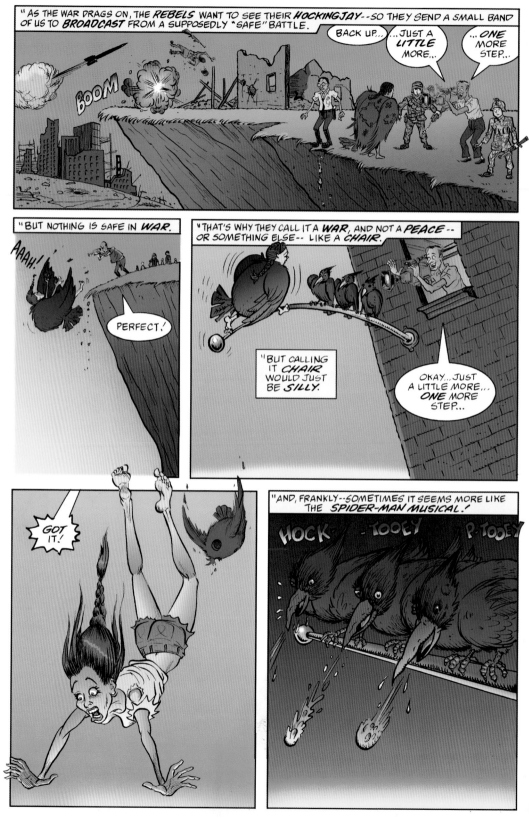

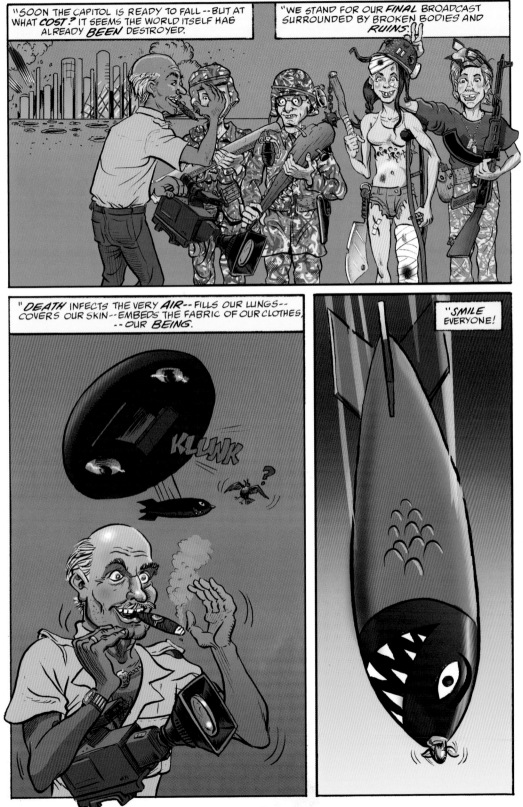

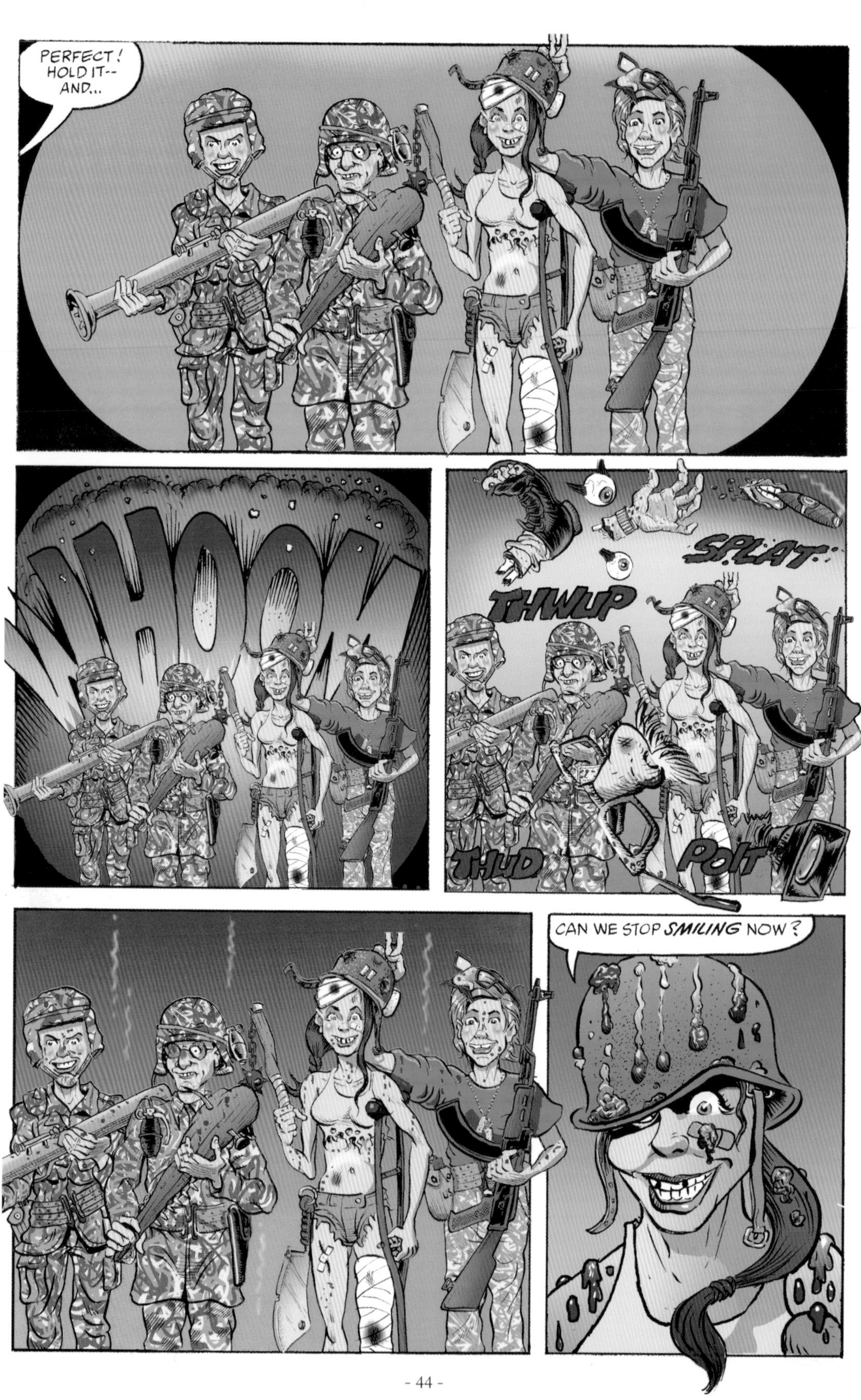
PERFECT! HOLD IT-- AND...
WHOOM
THWUP
S.PLAT
THUD
POIT
CAN WE STOP SMILING NOW?

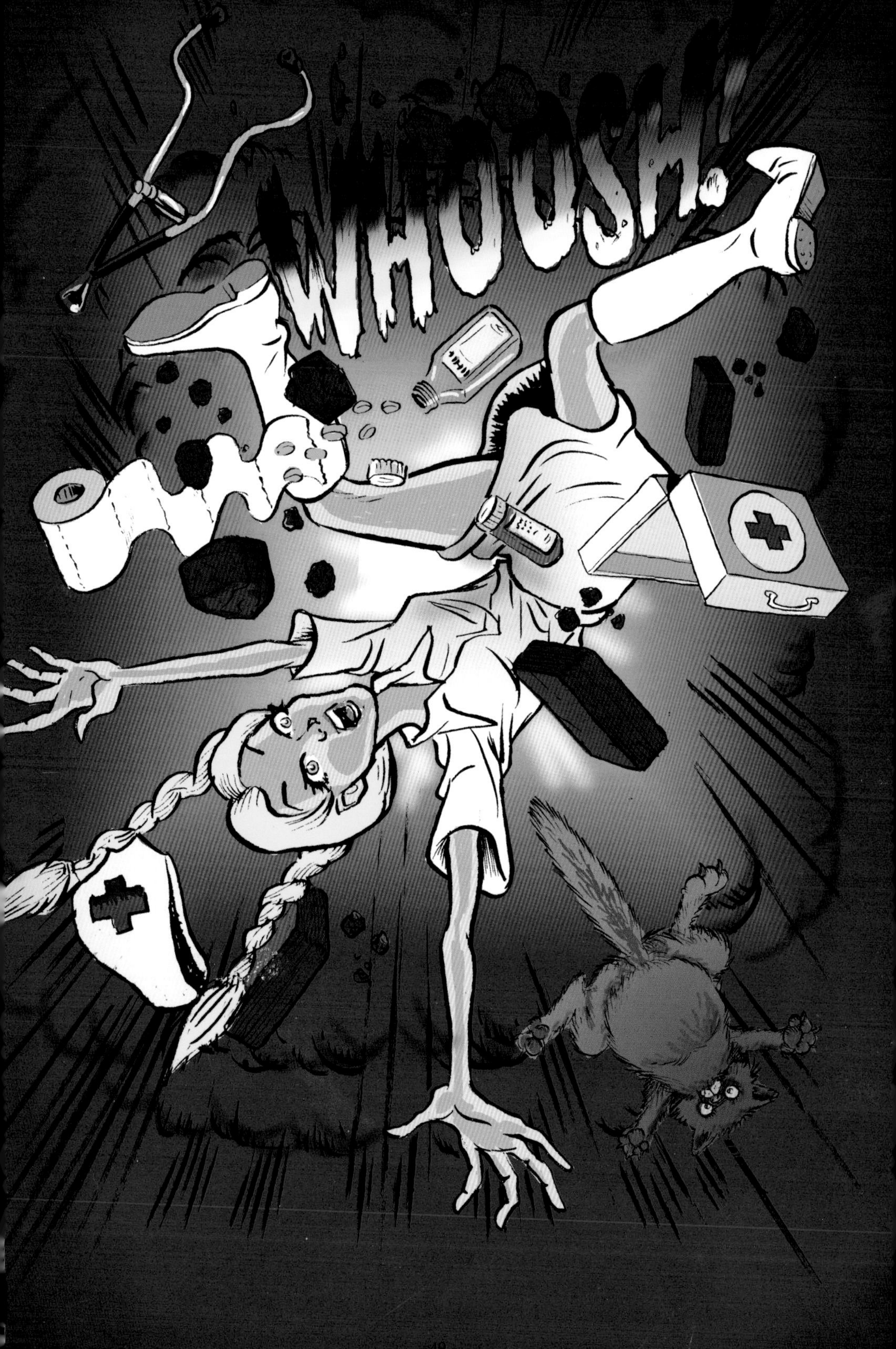
WHOOSH!

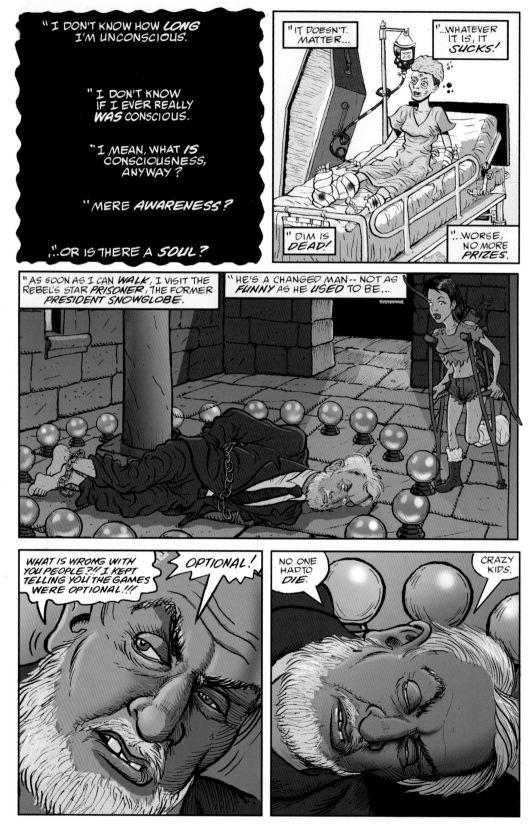

"OUR NEW PRESIDENT, *THELMA GROIN*, IS TRUE TO HER WORD. *I'M* TO BE THE ONE TO EXECUTE SNOWGLOBE.

"HEYBITCH AND FLAIL ARE TO BE AT MY SIDE.

"BUT WE ALL KNOW *WHO* SENT PEEKA TO KILL ME.

"*WHO* SENT DIM TO DIE.

"AND WE ALL KNOW *WHAT* I'M GOING TO DO.

"EXCEPT MAYBE *HEYBITCH*.

"THE *NEW* PRESIDENT ISN'T MUCH DIFFERENT FROM THE *OLD*.

"EXCEPT SHE'S A WOMAN, SHE'S BETTER DRESSED AND SHE HAS MY SISTER'S CAT, *BUTTERBUTT*, ON HER LAP.

"BUT THEN YOU GET INTO THAT WHOLE *WHAT IS CONSCIOUSNESS* QUESTION.

"OKAY, MAYBE SHE *IS* DIFFERENT.

"THERE HE IS, THE MOST *EVIL* MAN IN WHAT'S LEFT OF THE WORLD. I'M TO MAKE AN *EXAMPLE* OF HIM.

"WOULD IT BE ANY DIFFERENT FROM WHAT HE DID TO ME? ANY DIFFERENT FROM THE *GAMES?*

"YEAH...

"*THIS* TIME THERE *AREN'T* ANY PRIZES!"

"I *KNOW.*

"I DON'T KNOW *WHAT* FLAIL IS THINKING, PROBABLY THAT I'M PAYING TOO MUCH *ATTENTION* TO *SNOWGLOBE* NOW.

"I ASKED.

"*TWICE!*

"I DON'T CARE *WHAT* HEYBITCH IS THINKING.

WATCH OUT FOR PAPERCUTZ™

Welcome to the facetious, felicific, and frightfully feral fourth volume of PAPERCUTZ SLICES, the critically acclaimed graphic novel series dedicated to painfully poking fun at your favorite pop culture phenomena. I'm Jim Salicrup, the son of a ditch-dweller and Papercutz Editor-in-Chief, here to thank you for buying this Papercutz graphic novel. You did buy it, didn't you? 'Cause if you didn't we'll hunt you down and kill you! Oh, it was a gift? Well, that's different. We won't kill you then. Although, you may die laughing at the all the jokes and funny pictures we managed to pack into this edition of PAPERCUTZ SLICES. If you haven't read "The Hunger Pains" yet, and you're some kind of weirdo who reads the text pages first, perhaps you might want to consider taking out a life insurance policy…? You can even name me as your beneficiary. That only seems fair.

If this is the first time you've encountered PAPERCUTZ SLICES, that leads me to ask—where the heck have you been? You missed the hilarious "Harry Potty and the Deathly Boring," the vampire and werewolf-filled "breaking down," and the mythical "Percy Jerkson and the Ovolactovegetarians," all by the satirical team supreme, Stefan Petrucha (and co-writers and daughters Maia Kinney-Petrucha and Margo Kinney-Petrucha) and Rick Parker. Stefan and Rick first rocketed to farcical fame in the pages of TALES FROM THE CRYPT #8 which featured their "Diary of a Stinky Dead Kid"! And they've been lampooning together ever since.

Now, there's no need to get even the slightest bit depressed about missing these landmark accomplishments in the highly specialized field of spoofery and unauthorized parody, 'cause each and everyone one of these PAPERCUTZ SLICES comic masterpieces is still available at your favorite bookseller (you know—bookstores, online booksellers, comicbook stores, book fairs, etc.) or directly from Papercutz (see details on page 2). There's even a special boxed set, featuring all three of the previous PAPERCUTZ SLICES volumes available now! And if that wasn't enough, we've got a super special announcement to make in the very next paragraph…

Super Special Announcement: Due to popular demand, you can now order every volume of PAPERCUTZ SLICES digitally from comiXology.com. Whether you have an iPad or a Kindle Fire or one of a gazillion other digital devices, you can now enjoy "Harry Potty," "Percy Jerkson," or even "Diary of a Stinky Dead Kid," digitally. So, that should make all you gadget geeks super-happy!

So, while we still have your attention, may we direct it to the Papercutz excerpts and previews on the following pages…? We figure if you liked the mindless mayhem of "The Hunger Pains," then you'll love the Spinjitzu action in the pages of LEGO® NINJAGO. It's on sale now and available at booksellers everywhere. LEGO® NINJAGO features the exciting tales of four ninja battling the craziest foes you've ever seen. Written by Greg Farshtey, and illustrated by Paulo Henrigue, it's ninjas in the LEGO® style!

There's no room left to tell you what'll be Stefan and Rick's target for PAPERCUTZ SLICES #5, so you'll have to keep an eye on www.papercutz.com for future announcements. So, until we meet again-- May the Farce be with you!

Jim

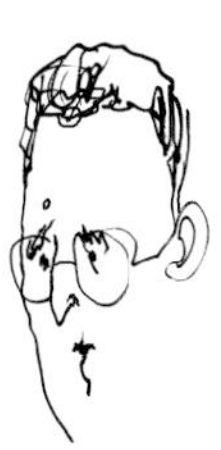

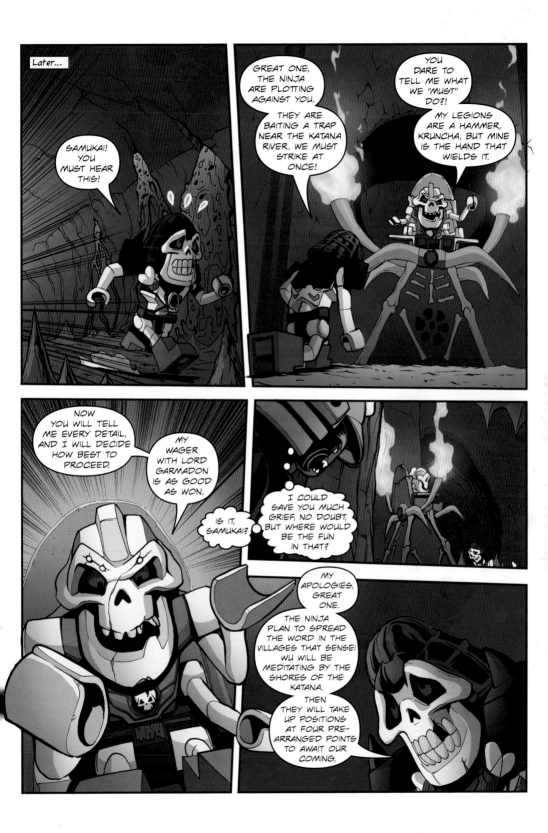

To be continued in LEGO® NINJANGO #1
"The Challenge of Samukai!"

LOTS MOE FUN!

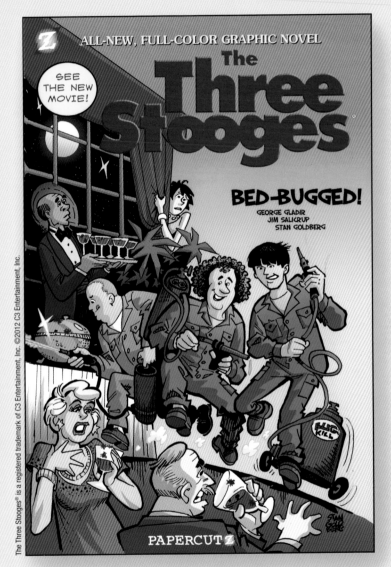

PLUS: LARRY AND CURLY FUN AT NO EXTRA COST!

Available Now at Booksellers Everywhere!

Think Inside the Box
Get the Boxed Set of Papercutz Slices #1-3!

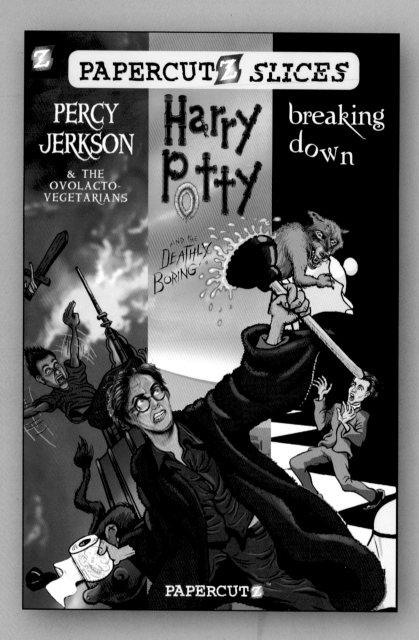